The Idea Which Thinks Itself

G.W.F. Hegel (1770-1831)

A NOVEL BY

Jon Foyt

The Idea Which Thinks Itself

Copyright © 2021 Jon Foyt

ISBN: 978-1-7333522-5-3

Published by

Big Hat Press
Lafayette, California
www.bighatpress.com

WHO IS JON FOYT?
And how can he have written this weird book?

Yes, he's an old white man from Indianapolis, but with plenty of experiences in his 89-plus years, plus a runaway imagination fed by hyperphantasia.

He attended the same high school as Kurt Vonnegut, a few years later.

He's lived in most parts of the U.S., including the Central Valley, where he experienced much of what is in this book.

He's built homes, too, worked in banking, electronics, and managed radio broadcasting in Oregon and Idaho.

He's studied Buddhism, and been a Presbyterian.

He's been in the Armored Corps of the U.S. Army and in Military Intelligence during the Koran War.

He went back to college in Georgia and studied the Confederacy.

He's experienced a host of medical problems plus the passing of his wife and many friends.

He's lived in two retirement communities before moving to Rossmoor where he has been head of the Stanford Club plus seeing the historic beacon atop Mount Diablo from where the Central Valley climate zone can be felt.

Along the way, he's completed 60 full length marathons plus innumerable shorter races.

And he's written this, his 18th novel, for you to comment on.

He'll deliver to you a signed copy at a discount price in response to your email request to jonfoyt@mac.com

DEDICATION

To Helen, as always

The Idea, as unity of the Subjective and

Objective Idea, is the absolute and all

truth, the Idea which thinks Itself.

- Hegel 1830

CONTENTS

———

BOOK 2

PROLOGUE

───

The Great Central Valley of California, an unusually elongated and wide inland expanse, is cradled by the towering Sierra Nevada Mountain Range on its East and by the never-ending Coastal Range on the West. Given its economically strong agronomical attributes, this Valley could be a state unto itself, even a country, or so some say, perhaps even its own planet orbiting its own star—each Agricultural by name—a universally productive region serving its fertile farming function.

The Valley's unique climate zones birth their own brand of fog, called "tule" by the early-arriving Spanish, a name derived from the tall grasses growing everywhere. Moisture rising from those grasses forms a pervasive mist competing for dominance with the insistent sea fog blowing east over the coast of California from the vast Pacific Ocean. In a conflict never to be resolved, the two natural fog phenomena ascend Mount Diablo toward Charles Lindberg's beacon, installed a century ago to guide pilots of the fledging US Air Mail service on their route toward the East.

"Hold on!" Heck exclaimed, interrupting me, before elaborating, as he was wont to do, *"You're off our track here. We're not exploring 'Lucky Lindy' or his revolving..."* He paused, inserting, *"...even though you served on the committee to restore the antique beacon...we are not talking about U. S. airmail delivery, or Lindbergh's solo flight across the Atlantic, as important as it may have been, or as was the advent of airmail delivery for our people."*

"We?" I blurted.

"Yes, Lindberg's book. You of course have read his book. But why did you read it?"

I paused to think about Heck's critique of my mention of Lindbergh's book-long narrative. I've always liked Heck. He's my companion, only on occasion, not always, for Heck comes and goes like a cool summer breeze on a hot humid afternoon, welcomed and then, having expressed itself and gone, its return being longed for.

But I must answer Heck's question of why I read Lindbergh's book. My reply flowed, "I wanted to get into his mind, to know the degree of self-discipline the daring aviator relied upon to fight off sleep, to navigate across the endless ocean, from the U.S. to France and to pilot his single-engine airplane solo, "The Spirit of Saint Louis," from the U.S. to France—and to be the first to fly across the Atlantic solo." I exclaimed, "My God, what courage!" I waited for Heck's anticipated ensuing endorsement. But there was only silence, as I acknowledged to myself that indeed I was off course.

Heck and I were outside a large convention-type hall waiting to participate in an all-male meeting, or whatever this group of men might turn out to be, to which I had been invited by Dave, my land surveyor friend and collaborator in several Central Valley housing developments. Those were the ones that worked, but also included attempts that failed to receive planning commission approvals—not to mention the ones where the houses were so slow to sell that profits were eaten up by on-going bank interest as some developments proved so slow to sell as to be a treadmill to nowhere. Alas, I knew— and Dave did, too—the financial risks of trying to make a living in real estate. Therefore, for potential profit's sake for whatever development I would be pursuing following this days' get together, I must focus on the gathering at hand—the present moment with its potential opportunities for my future—while retaining and enhancing the business friendship of Dave, my surveyor friend.

BOOK ONE

CHAPTER 1

Heck

———

He calls me "Heck." That's not my name. In fact, I have no name, but he calls me Heck, and we converse in depth. I mean our talk is not surface or superficial, and sometimes it really goes deep. He's rather smart, but—I'll let you in on my take—I'm a bit smarter. That's why he talks to me, and I to him. And we get along, at least I think so, because he keeps conversing with me, and I with him.

Other men, who are like him, are rumored to talk to their own personal imaginary friends. I know that, but the other men don't know I know. The reason I know is that I talk to the friends of the other men, and they to me. That is, whenever we do get together. Me and them. You see, each of us belongs to the I-O-I-F.

"What's that, you ask? Read on, I implore."

* * *

As to this vast valley, in a distant prehistoric time, our human ancestors migrated here and began to populate the area, from the Wintuns to the Ohones in the middle, along with other indigenous cultures from other regions of what would eventually become California. Over time, actually in quite recent times, came the arrival of the Spanish, along with the Portuguese, the Basques and their sheep, and then those greedy Easterners from New York and all those places whose men were seeking gold "out west" and the personal wealth it would bring them.

So, in the age before the transcontinental railroad was conceived and completed, these eager, and some say foolhardy, men made their way to the foothills of the Central Valley of California, more specifically to what was called "The Mother Lode." To get there, they came either by sailing around Cape Horn (all the time on their journey fearing shipwreck and drowning), or by foot and maybe horse across the Isthmus of Panama (with each moment fearing the yellow fever and/or malaria, or possibly being hacked to death by warriors of one or more of the 26 indigenous tribes). Each Eastern person dared defy these dangerous hurdles of the day in their wanton eagerness to seek gold near Fort Sutter. That outpost had been established by the invading Eastern Yankees who soon coveted the area and all the lands for miles around, finally grabbing all this land from Mexico by means of the 1848 Treaty of Guadalupe-Hidalgo ending the Mexican War.

Declaring their own Bear Flag Republic, they gathered in a plaza, the size and dimensions of which were decreed by the King of Spain, who had once ruled these lands but lost out in the Mexican Revolution of 1820. The king's territorial loss was followed by the rulers of Mexico in their ill-conceived and lost war against the westward-moving Manifest Destiny Americans. Alas, for the government in Mexico City, the Treaty called for them to give up title to what would promptly become Alta California, along with the U. S. states of New Mexico, Nevada, Arizona, and part of Colorado.

In California their loss included the Great Central Valley. That meant the many Mexican Land Grants given to political and wealthy prominent Mexicans were eligible to be incorporated into the new state of California after the vast area became a state and entered the Union in 1850.

Today this same valley might be labelled "Agricultural Valley," for that is what it is and does. However, given the economic impact of The Great Depression of the 1930's, academics came to label the area "a vast rural slum." Yet today, these lands have become a valuable product of its fertile soil, which is annually nurtured by the spring water tumbling down in streams, and artesian flows from the melting snow pack atop the western slopes of the Sierra Nevada Mountain Range. From the fertile fields of this valley, the many diverse agricultural products feed the nation and the world. Its farming technology is among the most advanced anywhere, thanks to the creativity and innovation conceived and expressed in its techniques and advanced machinery produced by the state's agricultural college.

Listening, Heck nodded his agreement.

CHAPTER 2

The Hall and the Men Entering

*I believe in Liberty for all men: the space to reach
their arms and their souls,
The right to breathe and the right to vote,
The freedom to choose their friends, enjoy the sunshine,
And ride on the railroads, uncursed by color, thinking, dreaming,
Working as they will in a kingdom of beauty and love.*

- W.E.B. DuBois (1868-1963)

———

The Tule fog engulfs, then lifts ever so slowly, revealing the multi-garbed ingredients of the valley, such as its grocery store food basket of crops and from its bordering foothill and mountainous lands, grazing goats, sheep, and cattle populate. Here I was today, standing at the edge of the large parking lot outside this convention hall, toward which and into which many men, their vehicles having been stowed, were now streaming toward and entering.

Heck and I were waiting in anticipation for my surveyor friend Dave's arrival. From the parked vehicles, the size, color, and make of their vehicles seeming to have outwardly defined them, men had been emerging. However, the sum total of their physical appearances would fail to draw a common denominator of physiognomy, for many ethnic traits were evident. In short, they represented a popery of Americana derived from the DNA legacy descended from five centuries of coming together on a new continent of immigrants from every continent and islands afar. In this New World, they had mixed with the in-place indigenous inhabitants. In short, every man was wearing a sartorial uniform, some tailored or some sloppy, each with the same mythical logo emblazoned across it, that being "American Male Past and Present." Were they each to be asked, the lot might respond by saying they were trying to run or help run a business, or an organization, or a congregation from a place of holy worship. Should they be queried further, they might explain to the interviewer that they were participants in a decades-old newly formed governmental plan in a society made up of adventurers and dreamers. Or, they might reply they were simply trying to make a living for themselves on behalf of their families, and perhaps even their grandchildren.

Stickers I spied on their vehicle' bumpers and windows more fully characterized each individual man. One displayed a political campaign slogan from yesteryear, "I like Ike." Across a chrome plated bumper was a playboy bunny in alluring costume, another suggested God was with us all. A bug screen on a massive pick-up truck proclaimed, "Jesus Is Coming." I waited in anticipation, but from the approaching vehicle appeared only another clean-shaven man in overalls greeting me with, "How the fuck are you, Good Buddy?"

Not knowing the driver but wishing to be cordial, I smiled and did a thumb's up, holding out my hand to shake, which we did as I told him my name and he told me his. My new buddy volunteered, "I hear we're in for a special guest today...know who?"

Shaking my head negatively, I replied, "No, haven't heard."

As he pulled open one of the double glass doors on his way inside, he turned toward me and speculated, "Someone important from Washington." And he went inside.

I nodded at some of the men and they returned my cursory greeting. And then from out of the fog, his favorite Leica total station in hand, strove Dave. We did a high five as I expressed my thanks for his invitation to attend the event.

"You'll not be sorry," Dave assured me as he put his arm around my shoulder. Side by side we entered the vast community hall through the automatically-opening double glass doors. "This is our point of beginning," Dave advised, using a surveying term I recognized—the point where your investigation begins and opportunity becomes the theme. Mine, hopefully, was about to unfold… maybe….

I felt glad Heck was close by. *"Cool,"* he commented. Then *"Ouch,"* as he exclaimed, *"In the thick fog, I hit my head on a wall I could not see."*

In prophecy, I whispered, "Heck, my friend, today there will be lots of walls we cannot see."

"The fog of our lives, you mean?"

I nodded. "Mine" I said and repeated, "Mine. Oh, yes, yours, too, Heck…ours."

CHAPTER 3

The New Farming

—

Wanting to see the new local agricultural techniques of farming and its accompanying techniques first hand, during one long day recently, Heck and I, with equal amounts of curiosity and admiration, had observed the ongoing one-day scenario of a large farming tract.

Arriving at dawn, per Heck's instructions, we watched the choreography of, first, the arrival of a land armada of giant machines that promptly began, row by row, to cruise slowly across the entire acreage harvesting in full the ripened crop. In the process, each machine automatically deposited the vegetable crop into its tag-along truck, filling the truck's bed to capacity. As it left, another empty truck arrived and, in turn, played tag with the huge harvesting machines in anticipation of a fresh load of produce to haul away and deliver to the market or a packing house.

Heck said he didn't think it made any difference whatever the crop was, because in the season of each and every conceivable crop, the same process would be repeated. That is, except for the crop of pecans and almonds that would see the new invention of machines designed to violently shake the trees so that the fruit would fall into the tarpaulins spread beneath the branches.

Hours later, as we observed the action across our field, the entire crop having been harvested, loaded, and trucked away, a new armada of agricultural battleships appeared. They floated in and set to work plowing the entire acreage, all the while collecting what was left of the roots of the previous crop and depositing the compostable debris into a fresh series of following trucks.

Mid-day, the orchestrated process was readying the field for the next crop planting. *"All of all these events have occurred in just one long day,"* Heck explained, to me, as if by now I hadn't figured it all out. But he wanted me to understand.

Next came more machines planting the seeds of the next crop, followed by bursts of nurturing irrigation water pumped to the surface from the aquifer, thus stimulating the scenario sequence of another crop growing cycle.

CHAPTER 4

The Hall

A man must make his opportunity, as oft as he finds it.

- Francis Bacon (1561-1626)

———

Entering the huge hall with Dave and seeing all the men greeting each other and talking, my thoughts considered: In these turbulent times, when everyone seems to take opposing and belligerent sides on almost every issue, a person, like you and me (and Heck), engages preferably with either friends or, as required, with enemies. Same can be said for the media, for when we choose a side and/or make our selection, we open our lives to inspection and judgment from those who may be observing us. Yet, in order for us to explore the world, and to carry out our personal assignments, we must either confront an opponent or soothe ourselves by clinging to a selection to which, in comfort, we always subscribe. Our opinion choice most always seems to lead us to confront or agree with an opinion friend. In making our choice, we fall either into or out of our own comfort zone of thought. It's that simple. "Isn't that so, Heck?"

I've never known Heck to be flippant, quick to anger, or to fire off an opinion. So, when Heck didn't respond right away, I was not concerned. Instead, he seemed to be mulling over my circumspect observations. That is unusual for someone to do in this day and age, for when someone rings a controversial bell, the Pavlovian response of the other is generally immediate, producing either the expression of an opposite point of view or one that is tried, true. But opinions do fly in both directions, like two opposing naval warships when, upon seeing each other, they immediately fire on each other, to the death, for sure in such matters.

Here in the hall, however, as I observed the groups of men standing or sitting at various tables, I saw no arguing, only nods of heads or what seemed like friendly banter or serious conversation. Could it be these men were not arguing, but rather were all on the same page, so to speak, discussing the same mission with both congeniality and mutual interest?

Perhaps, as Heck has said to me from time to time, if all the imaginary friends were to unite in a message of tolerance plus curiosity, the result might be a more open-mindedness on the part of the men and women of today's world. But Heck is Heck, and he is certainly not a conformist to the day's discordant Pavlovian rule du jour.

CHAPTER 5

Meeting the Men

Treat all men alike. Give them the same law.
Give them an even chance to live and grow.

- Chief Joseph

———

Now, as Dave and I surveyed the rapidly filling convention hall, Heck exclaimed, *"There's no speaker podium."* Before us stretched a concourse into which had been set a countless number of round tables in random arrangement, each with chairs assigned.

Heck's tone insisted I answer him as he renewed his comment, *"But where's the podium? Where's the speaker going to be?"* He added, *"There's not even a stage for performers. For sure, something's not right here."*

"There's no fix to fix," I observed. Heck acted confused, which he seldom does.

On his own, Dave offered, "As you can see, my friend, there will be no actors, no dancing girls, no vaudeville here tonight or to-morrow." Dave waited a brief moment for his words to sink in before adding, "This here is serious business."

"How long?" I asked.

"This afternoon. This evening. Tonight. Tomorrow."
I gulped. Heck whispered, *"Hot damn. I never...."*

* * *

The men continued moving into the hall from the parking lot, leaving behind their pickup trucks and sedans to roast in the sun or, many hoped, to wash in the purifying rain, which would help mitigate the effects of the prolonged drought. After all, each person knew, had they crops, which friends and relatives in this valley surely cultivated, without the precious nutrient of water there likely would be only stunted growth.

Motioning for me to follow, Dave led us first to one and then on to a number of other tables where men were talking. Some had opened a bottle of beer and begun sipping. A few laughed loudly. Dave addressed most of the men by name and introduced me to several.

"Meet Father Isadore. His is the most important sanctuary hereabouts," Dave clarified, "That is, as measured by the number of parishioners." The holy man smiled at me, and I shook his hand. He was dressed in his clerical garb, making me wish I also had a tailored uniform to designate my mission in life of developing tracts of bare land and building nice homes thereon. But too late. My die had been cast and for that I felt glad, but for my loss of immediate recognizable personal identity, I felt sad. Would that we each dressed according to our life's assignment. The military had solved that problem, I reflected, with style and fit of uniform, insignia affixed designating branch of service with rank as shown by stars, bars, or chevrons.

Such identification here today would take the guess work out of meeting the new people I found myself encountering in this grand convention hall. "Hello! Guess who I am and what I do in life."

"Wrong! Guess again." "Give up?" "Now I'll tell you. But who I am and what emotions I have and cope with daily will remain closeted behind my structured and practiced façade, forever and ever, Amen.

I wondered about the emotions of the priest. Was Fr. Isadore happy in his role in this valley, in this town, in his diocese? Perhaps any such emotional requirements varied according to the rules of the order to which he belonged. Appearing inwardly content with his holy mission, Fr. Isadore smiled warmly at the two of us and advised Dave, "We need more off-street parking, as I've told you before. I keep stressing that a filled parking lot is a turn-off for members of my flock. They arrive to worship expecting to park close so they have only a short distance to walk to worship."

Dave nodded and said, "Yes, Father, I am aware of your desires in this matter. One of our local developers, Bobby Turner, is working with me on convincing the owner of the abandoned K-Mart next door to your sanctuary to sell. Instead, the guy wants to offer your church a long-term lease."

"My bishop won't countenance that. He says the church must always own.

Having listened to the exchange, I decided to contribute my own thoughts. "Then, Father, may I suggest that you ask one of your benefactors to take up the lease, as offered? Then you can demolish the old store, grade the lot, pave it, and add the necessary striping to meet city parking code. That way your church will have adequate paved off-street parking 24/7. I suspected, however, that such a maneuver was probably already in his holy playbook. Nevertheless, he thanked me for the idea and said he would pursue it.

As the large room was nearing capacity, Heck whispered to me that he could feel the heartbeat of all the men present–not in sync, not in rhythm, not in unison, not in lockstep, but in a cacophony of vital human organs intent on reciting a popular melody, maybe a tune from the ancients, or perhaps not. Heck made one of his rare jokes, *"Like animals in heat."*

I corrected, "In heat, perhaps as in that emitted by their dominating business hormones."

"For once, you're right," Heck agreed.

Heck seldom complemented me, and I felt a surge of confidence.

Dave was moving on, and next introduced me to a man in quite different and unfamiliar attire. "Meet Marston Wright," he said.

Observing me with a stern but friendly face, Marston gestured to his Old World attire and remarked, "You're eyeing my customary traditional outfit. Let me fill you in. We Dukhobors are determined to retain our farming identity while making our students aware of the diverse backgrounds of the ethnic folks who populate the Central Valley. My ancestors came from Russia a hundred years ago to escape the Bolshevik Revolution. We abhor upheavals like that. Besides, we're not communists. Our ancestors were invited to come to Russia by Catherine the Great. She guaranteed us our safety and our customs. But then came the Revolution, and we were discriminated against. There aren't many of us here in the Valley. We dress differently from you, and we stick together, treasuring our cultural and religious values."

"Marston teaches ethics and civics in the high school," Heck advised. To my surprise, Heck went on, *"He's also on the Board of the local Junior College that has several agricultural degree programs."*

I asked Marston if the high school had sufficient funds to support his civics teaching program.

Shaking his head, he replied, "Far from it." He then explained, "The Good Lord cannot convince the taxpayers to vote in favor of parcel taxes. You know, those are the taxes that pay for educational programs in high schools and junior colleges. Long term bonds—the money voted in special elections to approve bonds to build the physical facilities. That they understand, but they do not support taxing their land and houses to pay for teacher salaries and teaching supplies. So, the state's educational money, what there is of it, flows to Silicon Valley and Orange County where school superintendents and active voters carry more clout." He went on, "The result is that without a proper operating budget for our schools here in the Valley, our ability to deliver quality education to our young people falls short."

Marston moved away to talk to a tall lean, somewhat younger man with plastered down greying brown hair, and no hint of impending baldness. I saw the two shake hands and heard Marston utter the word "Congress." Then their ongoing conversation was lost in the growling hub-bub of male voices.

Dave filled me in, "That's Randy Rhodes. He's the staff assistant for our district's Congressman in Washington D. C.—grew up here, and heads the Congressman's local office as well as serves as his chief staff person—very important job, right behind the Congressman himself."

I could sense Heck frowning as he reacted, *"The long, long reach of our federal government back East in Washington shows up even here—three thousand miles away."*

Before I could make an attempt to talk to Randy Rhodes, Dave was leading me to another table to introduce me to a bulldog of a man who he said his name was Heinz Volk. "Manages our local branch of the People's National Bank." Dave added, "Sympathetic to real estate developers. On construction loans, allows adequate repayment time given the strict local jurisdictional regulations governing development. Plays by the book, German you know. Strict, no B.S. allowed."

Heck mused, *"Fair and square to deal with. Valuable intro from Dave."*

I smiled at the banker. Volk looked at me, rather through me, ranking me, I sensed, into one of his several classes of credit worthiness, concluding most likely that I was decidedly not a mainstream player possessed of big bucks to entrust to his bank.

Heck advised, *"Find a common ground with him—right now!"*

I asked, "Mr. Volk, did you grow up here in the Valley?"

He looked at me, and I felt as if I were being judged by his credit committee. I kept my attention focused on him. When he smiled, he seemed to be wrestling with what to say to me, then slowly he began to answer my question. "In 1939, right before the war started, my grandparents were able to get exit visas from Nazi Germany along with many others. Most sought a sort of sanctuary in the open city of Shanghai. They remained there as refugees during the war, even under eventual Japanese occupation."

I marveled at his story as he continued, "When World War II ended, my parents were soon able to leave China. My family had been given an endorsement from a relative in the U.S. Actually, several relatives who had come to the U.S.in one of the many early waves of German immigrants came forward and endorsed my family for entry and U.S. citizenship."

I asked, "How did you end up here in the Central Valley?"

He smiled, presumably indulging my curiosity. "My wife Elsa has relatives. We have a small German Jewish community here. The food, our food, you know, is so good." He pointed a finger toward me, "Say, you a German boy?"

"My father—"

"—I thought so. You better come into the bank so we can get better acquainted. Have lunch, you know." Volk laughed. "Open an account. Deposit lots of money that I can then loan out to one or more of these businessmen here today and, in the process, make money for my bank."

"Hoping the bank's money gets repaid," I suggested, and Volk and I laughed. Heck, too.

Volk made a circle with his middle finger and told me, "I want to keep banking as it was."

"How's that?" I. asked.

"Today, large national banks are centralizing everything while trying to save money with fewer branch employees, even fewer branches that are staffed by entry-level employees. If you have a banking question, they connect you by phone to a central office. I'll never do that never in my branch," Volk assured me.

Heck said, *"Tell him, you'll see him."*

That I did.

* * *

Turning to Dave," I asked, "What's our program for the rest of the day?"

"Have a beer…or two, or not, my friend. It's up to everyone. That is, who they talk to and what they talk about with other businessmen and community leaders participating in our large group. There's plenty of time for everyone to converse. It's deal day and tonight, as well—hopefully so for everyone." Dave scribbled numbers as if with an imaginary pen and drew a line across an imaginary sheet of paper and said, "The bottom line is that a lot of deals will be made here today, tonight, and cemented tomorrow before the guys return to their families and work places."

Dave went on to expound on the purpose of the business confab. "In this hall, my friend, the town and region of the Central Valley are run, whether that be local government, charities, schools, factories, wineries, churches, or the farms—all make up the backbone of the valley. That's what's all playing out here right now in this hall. Ths is where these men come together once a year, hopefully to make money for themselves, their families, and for the futures of their children and grandchildren." He added, "Indeed, for the year ahead, and even more years ahead." He concluded with, "By now I am sure you know how the American Capitalistic business drill marches forward, eh?"

At Heck's suggestion, I quoted President Calvin Coolidge, "The business of America is business."

Volk, overhearing, nodded. He pointed his finger at me and reassured me, "You are welcome here."

A somewhat older fellow, with beard and mustache and carrying a small leather bag, edged closer. Dave introduced me to "Louis Singer, M.D."

"Need any pills?" asked the doctor with a hearty guffaw, adding mischievously, "I also operate...you know, with the knife." He looked more closely at me, "But you look quite healthy." The doctor laughed again, playfully punching Dave in the gut and asked, "Why'd you bring him if he doesn't need any meds?"

I laughed. Singer smiled and moved on to confront Randy Rhodes, the Congressman's deputy I'd not yet met. The two engaged in a round of playful banter, and I saw the aide gesticulate as if he were pantomiming the rigid layout of the 435 desks that were assigned to the voting members of the U. S. House of Representatives.

Dr. Singer rubbed his hands together, "Must be quite a demand in that august hall back east in Washington, I should think." He laughed loudly, only to be playfully reprimanded by the aide, "Oh, no, doctor, those men and the few women members are as pure as New England driven snow."

I had to suppress Heck's monstrous belly laugh.

A burly man bellowed at Dr. Singer, "Good doctor, I've warned you enough times about dispensing those pills of yours without a prescription. Next time I'm going to—"

"—Yes, Sheriff Tony Rust, and how many pills for you today?" From those who overheard, lame snickers from all around.

Next Dave introduced me to Maxwell Lerner. "Max is dean of our local junior college."

A serious looking man, Lerner was younger than I would have expected a college dean to be. We shook hands, and I noticed his grasp was strong. Perhaps, I guessed, from years of working on a farm, herding animals and running machinery. Briefly, Max told me about his degree program for young men and women in agricultural economics, with an up-to-date introduction to the many new technologies of farming. "We're on the cusp of increasing agricultural production by leaps and bounds here in the Central Valley," he said, continuing, "We work closely with the state's agricultural four-year college. I find it all very exciting. Just think, we're feeding the world…well…you'll have to excuse me, as I get carried away with the merits of my educational mission. But that's what makes our Central Valley--this bastion of agriculture—so exciting and challenging…especially these days. You know, we're losing our dairies as the price of milk goes down, what with consumers drinking so much soy and almond milk." He shook his head in a show of despair.

Heck said, *"We need more men like Maxwell."*

I agreed and was about to comment to Maxwell when a serious-looking man in thin tie and sport coat came up to me, interrupting my conversation with Maxwell. In a sober tone, he introduced himself as Calvin Wright, pastor of the United Evangelical Church. Following the exchange of proper religious-type greetings, the minister motioned me aside and clamped a firm grip on my arm. In a low and conspiratorial tone, he issued his advice, "You're new here." I nodded. "Be very careful, with all these men, I mean, of the laying on of hands or other physical contact with any of them. You see, we simply cannot have any outward display of inter-male affection. This here's the Central Valley, not Castro Street in wayward San Francisco." He stared at me as if his ministerial job depended on my proper response. Stunned, I remained silent, wondering how to diplomatically counteract his prejudice.

Rev. Wright waited a moment for my consent. Not receiving it, he tugged at my arm and once more said, "Do you get my drift? I mean, do you know what I mean? Surely you do."

Dutifully, I nodded, wanting to be polite and not make an enemy of the minister, yet inwardly I was repelled. His judgmental mission having been explained, he seemed relieved, soon turning and searching, I presumed, for another male target to save from what he regarded as an awful male sin.

Heck, too, acting both surprised and disappointed, said, *"Men of some faiths are bound by their cult's mandatory sacred vows to carry out the policies of the head office officials in charge of their dogma's declarations and policies. Unfortunately, the headquarters people live not with reason and compassion, as taught in the Bible and other holy books, but rather in the biases and dogma of those who have run and are running the religion, having been indoctrinated in their vows with what they are told to believe to be their religion's divine mission."*

Heck was being overly learned, but I excused my imaginary friend as, on occasions such as this, he being quite opinionated about religion. I did wonder, however, how a world-wide organization kept its members in tow, or for that matter how countries maintained at least an outward stance or popular appearance of their adopted policies in locations outside of their own defined borders. Could they do so without caving in to dissident elements? Maybe it was the threat of personal punishment, or the fear of being ostracized from one's own chosen group or profession that kept people in line and their behavior disciplined to the prescribed cause.

Here in the giant hall, no one that I could see was suffering any consequences from the minister's admonitions, nor were they taking time to disagree with him. The reason was that everyone was on today's intent and commonly-agreed upon male mission of making money. All other topics were subordinate in importance, at least in most cases, or so I was coming to realize.

It was then that a man holding a brochure came up, unfolding it for me to see the Acropolis as he gestured at its famous Parthenon high atop. Implying his knowledge of all the history embedded with it, and asking if I wanted in on a real special travel deal to Greece, he told me, "It's a small intimate trip I've arranged just for men of this community to enjoy with their wives." He said his name was George Goforth, appropriate I thought, for advocating his money-making, or was it my money-saving deal. I felt Heck chuckle.

"I've been there," I told him. "I recall joining other tourists waiting in anticipation to exit our particular tour bus after it had vied for a scarce parking space down below the Acropolis."

George held up his hand as if to deter me from voicing any further travel frustrations. "The trick in successful travel," he advised, "is to filter out the noise and commotion around you and focus on your tour guide's description of the history or the architecture of what you are seeing."

"*Good advice for travelers who want to learn,*" Heck commented.

I agreed, thanked George and told him I would consider his special trip offer.

It was then that I saw Dave earnestly engaged in what seemed a rather deep conversation with a guy wearing a corduroy jacket. An unlit pipe shinny from heavy use was tucked upside down, its empty bowl facing outward from his coat's handkerchief pocket. Dave motioned to me to approach, and I did as Dave said, "Meet Jim Early, manager of our radio station KROP and KROP-TV, plus City Editor of our newspaper, *The Daily Harvester.*"

I could feel Heck becoming excited.

Dave whispered to me, "Jim's just picked up a rumor, something federal—"

The journalist interrupted, "Not verified, to be sure. Our paper must have two sources before we take a rumor with any degree of seriousness and consider assigning either a newspaper reporter or a television journalist to investigate.

I spoke out, "I understand the rules for reporting, having studied journalism in school. So, tell me, Jim, what is this hot rumor?"

"Rule applies," the editor advised.

"But you just shared it with Dave here," I protested and then urged, "So, could you let me in on the secret."

"Sharing with Dave doesn't count."

Heck critiqued, *"Double standard."*

I agreed with Heck but, with my curiosity rising, I didn't know what to say. Silence. Then I asked, "At least you can tell me your source?"

No reply from Jim, but Dave gestured toward the Congressman's aide who was standing nearby. Must have been from him, I ventured a guess to myself.

I sensed Heck agreeing with me.

Just then an athletic-looking man, tall and agile, rushed toward me, slowing to a stop in order to introduce himself as, "Hi there, I'm Lou Parnell, high school football coach, basketball, too," continuing with an explanation by way of his dual coaching responsibilities, "No money for separate coaches. Some money, however, for Title IX so women can play, as well. Long overdue, I say, but not all the voters in the district agree with me. Some persist in advocating we stick with traditional roles for girls—like home economics. Wrong, I tell them, athletic opportunities are for each gender."

Dave and I added our verbal support with Heck chiming in, *"About time for women."*

With a proud smile on his weathered face, Lou told me, "I'm descended from a long line of Irish revolutionaries, Parnells of course. That's where I get my non-conformism."

Lou and I shook hands and I asked him how his season was going. His eyes lit up as he boasted, "I've devised this new play my football team is practicing. It is really going to confuse our opponents. I guarantee it."

I expressed interest, having played some football myself back then.

"Well," Parnell began, "on our first offensive play, our team lines up in usual formation, except—"

"—Except?" I prodded.

"Except, our center lines up as the left end."

"Why ever for?"

"Hear me out. You see that, as an end, this player becomes an eligible pass receiver. So, our new end hikes the ball to our halfback and then runs down the field, receiving the halfback's forward pass. By now the opponents are so confused they miss defending for the pass, and the center (our eligible receiving left end, of course) catches the pass and runs lickety-split down the field, crossing the goal line for a touchdown."

I protested, "Wait just a damn minute, Coach Lou, you must be violating several rules with your daring new play. The referee will surely immediately wave his arms frantically in the air, calling the play back and nullifying your score. Plus, he'll add a penalty of some amount of yardage for an illegal formation."

Coach Parnell waved off my protest by saying, "Show me in the high school football rule book where this is an illegal formation and play." Then forcefully he grabbed my shoulder and added profoundly, "Look, if every time someone in our society got a new idea, someone else would promptly find a passage in some dusty old rule book calling it illegal, thereby rescinding it and stifling progress and preventing change, where would our society be today? I mean, for example, can you un-do the Industrial Revolution as a rule book violation?"

I saw his point and said, "Some Luddites might like to return to the days and ways of yesteryear, in which they might feel more comfortable and less stressed by the onrush of new ideas, the changes in technology and the buffeting they experience in their comfort zone and way of life. Or so I had quickly suggested to the coach. But then I had to acknowledge that Lou Parnell had a valid societal point. I could only suggest he check out his new play and formation with high school football's headquarters, wherever that was.

Parnell thanked me, as Heck intoned, *"Coach Lou offers a valid point."*

I nodded as the Coach hurriedly dribbled-like away, maneuvering adeptly between and amongst the men, each high-fiving him as he passed.

* * *

By now, having benefited from Dave's multiple introductions, I had met and briefly, very briefly, spoken to a number of men, with still many more groups mingling throughout the hall, all remaining to be met. As we moved among the various clusters, I queried each man when appropriate, about his business or profession, while mentioning to some my own hope of building a few houses in the region. Not that, later on, could I recall everybody's name and the business or organization they owned or represented. I hoped that Heck would remember the names and occupations, given his prompting me, on occasion, as to what to say. With that input, I might at least nod as if I was on board to recognize and acknowledge each man I met as to his own personal agenda.

For the most part, I began to conclude that each man in the room was eager and ready to inform me of his recent life activities, along with his hopes for the future. However, all steered clear of revealing any fears in either their personal life or in the conduct of their businesses. Almost all were willing to happily disclose some praiseworthy thing about members of their families, especially their sons and how well they were doing playing little league baseball or Pop Warner football, so far without any serious injuries, other than….

Heck said, *"Believe me, Buddy Boy, each of these men have real fears, recurring doubts, and gnawing apprehensions. The myth that real men have no unsettling or even debilitating emotions is totally wrong."* He paused, but I knew he was going to say more on the subject, which he did, *"If men do suffer silently from unruly emotions, such as when a friend or family member becomes ill or even passes away, the ever-present male myth explains that such emotions are fleeting and are to be quickly hidden, set aside out of view of other males and certainly all females."* Heck waited for effect, was silent a bit longer before appending, *"But I'm telling you, these male emotions linger on in men's minds although they are usually covered up to the outside world."*

Then, changing the subject, Heck called my attention to how the men were dressed. *"Not formal, except for the priest over there. Maybe outdoorish. Not Sunday church. Except Heinz Volk"*—he pointed—*"he's their banker, evidence his three-piece suit and his icy-tinted glasses."*

"Yes, Heck, I talked with Volk, got invited to lunch."

I knew that news pleased Heck.

CHAPTER 6

The Marine Colonel

*The men who have succeeded are men who have chosen
one line and stuck to it.*

\- Andrew Carnegie

———

As I moved farther into the crowd of men, I found myself standing tall next to an imposing figure, who introduced himself to me, "Lt. Colonel Malcom Hammil." On his jacket, sewn into a lapel, stood out the familiar Marine Corps emblem. I saw that he saw that I saw, and he said, "Retired."

"What do you do in your retirement?" I asked.

Heck commented, *"He just told you—he's retired."*

"Good question," the colonel allowed. "One must always be doing something…right…even in retirement. In my opinion, retirement is not a do-nothing episode in one's life."

I nodded, and the Colonel went on, "Be constructive in your action, I always say."

"And that is to do?"

"I go to the Legion Hall a lot and other veteran organizations and advise soldiers about questions they raise as to their lives during retirement."

"Such as?"

"Though I'm not a doctor, I try to comfort them with their medical concerns, which are often PTSD. I talk to them about their visits to the Veterans Administration Hospital and other medical questions they may have. Also about money matters, maybe their marriages—you know, I was married for 60 years to my Lady. We moved from Marine base to Marine base, and eventually into a retirement community near here. That's where I live now.

"And your wife?"

"Passed on…but she and I will meet again in our special rendezvous in heaven."

Heck whispered, *"Sweet."*

CHAPTER 7

A Buddhist Physicist

———

It was at this juncture that I met Samuel Goldstein, as he was formally introduced to me by Dave who said, "Sam is the physics instructor at our high school," and Dave left it at that without further embellishment.

Lacking much common ground with a physics instructor, I asked, "Tell me, why are you here today, tonight, and maybe even tomorrow?"

He looked at me, perhaps annoyed at my simplistic question. Then, sensing my innocent curiosity, he replied, "One bit of advice as to male conversations, my friend, is to be careful with queries. For when you ask another man a question, often he may regard it as a display of your weakness." He explained his personal axiom further, "A societal myth is that real men have all the answers and have no need to ask questions of anyone." He paused and extended his thumb downward, saying, "That, of course, is bull shit. Each of us men, most of the time, do have questions, for which we really crave, and need, answers."

I was buoyed by his words, for the longer I was in this convention hall, the more questions I seemed to have, either expressed verbally or lodged in my mind.

I felt Heck nod.

With my eyebrows raised, I felt I was encouraging him to continue talking.

He went on, "My mission in this assemblage of soldiers of business—the pawns, so to speak, of American capitalism—is to introduce what might be a new or different slant to their discussions."

In anticipation, I hesitatingly asked, "Which would be?"

"Several Buddhist concepts."

"Are you a Buddhist?" I asked in surprise.

Dr. Goldstein merely smiled.

Stumped, I quickly recovered and queried, "Are you going to preach some sort of religious dogma to the men here?"

"No. One doesn't preach Buddhism," came the reply, "so the answer is 'No.'" smiling, he added, "One feels it."

Heck said, *"Press him."*

I looked intently at Goldstein and said, "You mentioned several concepts? What might they be?"

He replied, "If you are truly interested, let me set the proper venue."

I told him that I thought the venue was right in this oversized convention hall, but no, I quickly learned that Dr. Goldstein had another one in mind, about which he appeared ready to introduce. He began with two simple words, "Outer space."

I stared at him, taken aback, and waited.

I could sense Heck losing patience.

Goldstein promptly said, "Our scientists are exploring outer space. They are devising ways to land manned and womaned space ships on Mars, for example. What do you expect they will find there?"

Heck speculated, *"Little green men, maybe little orange women, each wanting to emigrate to America. But wait, maybe they are each criminals, rapists, and evil-doers."*

Ignoring Heck, I suggested, "I suspect you will offer some clues, or maybe answers, to other life sources in our Universe."

Goldstein elaborated, "We have clues already."

Heck persisted in his spoofing, singing, "*The little greenies are coming, the little greenies are coming, but contrary to what you may conclude, they're not sympathetic to the green men of Ireland, nor even the orange men of Northern Ireland.*"

"Or orange women," I communicated silently to Heck, and bade him refrain from his negative comments until we had heard the teacher in full.

"Clues?" I pressed.

"You see," Goldstein professed, "When you sense or feel Buddhist philosophies and guidelines for your life, your true self begins to explore the legacies of your ancestors, which have been automatically bequeathed to you."

"You mean, I didn't necessarily ask for these legacies?"

"For each of us, it is an automatic gift from out of the past. The legacy traits come to each of us, along with another concept— the impermanence of life itself."

I stood in silence as I tried to digest the man's barrage of thought-provoking ideas, or doctrines...or...what?

"One other concept, if you're still with me."

I nodded.

"You must recognize, acknowledge, and revere your true self." He looked at me intently. "Do you know...or maybe I should ask...have you met your true self?"

For the moment, I was once more taken aback.

Heck instructed me to re-focus, "*Now!*"

I feared Goldstein was growing impatient with my silence. Finally, I ventured, "It's not what others see. It is what I feel about myself."

He nodded, "Good start. It's what's tucked away inside you behind the public façade that other folks see."

Thinking back about my academic life, I recalled that prior to having built a number of homes, I had studied architecture. I wanted to learn the heritage of styles in American homes so that I was up to date on outward design, along with interior floor plans and the impressions that my designs might convey to buyers—an uncertain skill trait to be sure, but one that was necessary if the homes I built were to find buyers. I recalled an architectural period appropriate to Goldstein's query. I expressed it to him. It had been prominent in Washington, D.C. I said, "Dr. Goldstein, I believe you are talking about the architectural term 'facadism.'"

Smiling, he implored, *"Go on."*

Heck seemed skeptical. *"You better make this good, Buddy Boy."*

I recalled to Goldstein, "Facadism is the style of preserving a building's façade, that is, its outward face—what appears on its streetscape—while concurrently rebuilding its interiors. The inside is made to conform to today's standards of functions and contemporary styles, whether it be offices, hospitals, hotels, or retail space, or some other approved and zoned use. Its function will conform to the latest in technology, from social media to Internet access, to electrical codes, and to handicap requirements under the Americans for Disabilities Act."

Goldstein nodded and requested of me, "Can you now apply that concept to the men here in our convention hall?"

Heck whispered, *"What we see is their facades displayed and acted out in demeanor, conversations, goals, etc. But what lies behind—therein resides their true self."*

I repeated Heck's words to Dr. Goldstein. In response, he

shook my hand and said, "Think of this concept when you meet new people and begin to talk to them and try to explore the nature of their true self. Therein lies your conversational goal with each fellow human being. That, my friend, is your peek into Buddhism and your hope for understanding yourself and other persons here today."

I felt exhilarated and allowed, "Okay, I think I get it. Thank you." I paraphrased, "In other words, if we really want to know the true nature of a structure or a person, look behind its street-facing façade."

He said, "You got it. It's yourself entering a sort of enlightenment by going behind your public façade to see what's behind—that being your true self." Dr. Goldstein went on to tell me, "Given the huge number of people populating this globe today and their collective brain power, think of the new ideas being born every moment, the new ventures being launched, the new products being introduced. There are new horizons of science being investigated as we stand here. You need to catch a glimpse into the concept of impermanence that governs and changes our lives."

I asked, "How do we 'survive' so many changes?"

He advised, "Cling to the gunwale of your lifeboat and hang on, riding with the swells and incoming tides of ideas and thoughts."

CHAPTER 8

The Investment Broker

———

A man talking nearby to a group overheard Goldstein's advice and motioned to me to join his little confab. "We're talking about investment ideas—where to put the money you are each going to make here today and tonight," he began, quickly introducing himself as, "Alfonse Midcap," before turning back to his assemblage and continuing with his ideas, "To begin again, gentlemen, these bonds I'm about to tell you about are obligations and guaranteed by my firm. They pay a whopping 10 per cent interest, with monthly checks sent to you. The income is based on a collection of loans made by my firm—"

"—Which is?" someone asked.

Alfonso was quick to reply, "Guaranteed Savings and Loan." At this point he passed around colorful brochures describing his firm. On the back was his picture shown with several other men who were listed as corporate executives. "I can issue these bonds to you or to you or your business in increments as small as $ 5,000.00."

My surveyor friend Dave saw me listening to Midcap and came over. He pulled me aside, whispering, "These bonds have not been registered with the state securities office in Sacramento, so be careful." He added, "If you want to listen to some more respected investment advice, come with me now and I'll introduce you to Roger Goodfellow."

I followed Dave through the crowds and soon met Roger who told me right off, "I have 250 clients whom I advise regularly about their investments. We meet often to discuss their objectives."

Impressed, I asked, "How do you keep track of each investor?"

Heck commented, *"Important question."*

Roger replied, "I have a research team in San Francisco who keeps tabs on the stock market for me so that I can align my clients' needs with market conditions." He let that bit of information sink in and then asked, "Let's you and I schedule a 'get acquainted' meeting so that I can become more familiar with your requirements and objectives? He took out his pocket appointment calendar and announced, "We'll pencil in a date for lunch at the CVA club."

I stuttered to reply, stumbling out with, "I'm afraid, Roger, as to what I have…well, it is in mostly parcels of land in this region of the Central Valley. I intend to build some houses when I can get regulatory approval and financing."

With persistence, Roger said, "Well, clearly your situation will change as you build out your homes."

Heck said, *"Let's get on with it. Let's find out more about this rumor…."*

I thanked Roger and allowed as how me might meet again.

Heck said, *"But you don't know when, right?"*

I nodded.

CHAPTER 9

The Ancestors

Price, envy, avarice – these are the sparks that have set on fire the hearts of all men.

\- Dante Alighieri

———

Turning away, I found myself face to face with Samuel Goldstein once again.

The physics teacher looked at me, smiled and said, "One other thing."

"And that is?"

Goldstein continued, "You, and each of us, are beneficiaries of the legacy from our ancestors, our specifically inherited traits, shaded by our own take on our heritage and our understanding of our personal background. It's like evaluating a consumer product— that is, our heritage, which is stored on our personal shelf of life. When needed, when it helps us understand ourselves, we draw on it like a reserve stash of one's life savings."

Heck commented, *"Ancestor worship?"*

"Not worship," I told my secret friend, "No, Heck, I'm beginning to believe that rather it's trying to recognize your ancestor's traits, their skills, their lives, perhaps even their emotions."

Heck came back, *"But what if one of yours was a bank robber or a Nazi?"*

In my frown, I must have betrayed Heck's concern.

For Goldstein said, "I think I know what you may be thinking. For example, what if your ancestor was a Nazi?"

"Apologies," I offered, explaining, "It's my secret friend suggesting thoughts."

"Oh, yes, I have one, too.

"Male?"

"She's a she, I think, for she critiques my daily class lectures to my classes in the school here. Her comments help me in trying to reach the young and eager minds arrayed before me."

"You're not sure of your secret friend's gender?"

"Not a requirement these days."

Heck said, *"I know him or her."*

The teacher added, "But I must tell you, on my wife's side there was an uncle who was a prominent member of the Nazi party."

"And?"

"My wife's family was not Jewish, as of course was mine. Anyway, her uncle left us his memoires. My wife and I have read his writings and talked about him at length. We're trying to understand how having a monster for an ancestor impacts our values today."

I wanted to ask more, but then I saw Goldstein clenching his fist, his obvious expression of emotion deterring me from asking, "Did you learn what happened to him?"

Instead, he said, "We wanted to know, and we asked our counselor, thinking she might have answers to the basic legacy questions of what made him what he became and, as well, what unwelcome traits has our family inherited from him."

I did ask, "What judgment befell your wife's uncle?"

"Hung at Nuremberg."

With that, Goldstein was off, departing us, and was soon lost in the melee of men, leaving me and Heck to ponder his deep personal disclosure.

CHAPTER 10

Opportunity Knocks

———

Gradually, given Dave's personal introductions enhanced by Heck's observations and comments, I had developed a sense of what was playing out before me here in the convention hall. Those gathered had come with the hope of achieving certain business plans, or maybe they were as yet only ill-defined hopes or embryonic glimmers of thoughts about the future—the hopes of achieving one or more personal goals, the bottom line always being the jingle of adding more coins to those already in their pockets.

Slowly—maybe reluctantly, or maybe with anticipation, or maybe with the lure of achieving long-sought or newly conceived goals, they envisioned their achievements of today, tonight, and/or tomorrow. Many of the men, maybe most, believed they were or would be scoring big opportunities. Those hopes foretold of money through rewarding ventures. Successes would hopefully come their way if, in this hall, they were to strike the right lucrative deal with the right person that would benefit their business. In so doing, their families and especially the futures of their children and grandchildren would be assured.

Heck agreed with me, repeating, *"Lives being lived not only for themselves, but also for their wives, and especially for their progeny."*

In agreeing with Heck, I reminded myself that the things I had learned from living my own life with my own wife and two kids—the man, the father, the husband, the bread winner, the person with hoped-for male strength provides, and assures the wife that his planning is wholesome, strong, and made with good advice and good input from attorneys, accountants, and real estate advisors where and when appropriate, given one's particular circumstances. Isn't that one reason, perhaps the main reason, back then the to-be-wife had accepted his proposal of marriage?

Heck said he wasn't married and never wanted to be. *"That's for you romantics."* I sensed he was downplaying my perceived male role—evident in his tone.

I suddenly queried myself as well as Heck, given what I thought to be the typical male's motivations. Where was the real person hiding in what might be called the typical husband? Where was the true man, the father? Was he an octave above the one often photographed with a baby in his arms? Apart from his role of minding the money and charting the money maneuvers in his planning, where was the husband's true personal mind and values, his real behind the façade true self? Once described, was this mental money belt of his being honestly husbanded?

"He and his money are at work," Heck said as if everyone knew and understood that axiom.

I took issue right away with Heck. "Of course, he and his financial resources are employed, but what I now want to know is where is the husband's real self. I want to go beyond our discussion topics, and find out who is this typical man, what is his true self? Explore him here today, that is, meet and try to understand his true self, how different would his self be from the popular image the other men know him to be? And how different from the image he believes himself to be continually conveying to others? And how different and in what ways will that be from what he is perceived to be by members of his family?"

Heck was not saying anything for the moment. However, after a moment he suggested, *"There are many men like that here today. In this place, you and I have our chance, my friend, to encourage a number of men to come forward and tell us about their true selves."* But then Heck pulled up short, thought and queried, *"Where are such answers? We can't simply ask him to open his shirt and show us his true self in the same way he might want to display a scar from an operation by producing for show for us an in-depth clinical psychological profile case study, suitable for inclusion in some clinical think tank study."*

For a moment I worried my pursuit might be unrealistic, ill-conceived, and moreover a waste of time. I said, "I mean, isn't our answer that no one knows themselves in depth?" Heck and I remained silent for a little while before I dared to speculate, "But what if everybody showed their scars for some vivid Super Market display color scandal sheet, so to speak?"

Heck laughed at me, which upset me, and then he said *"What? You mean they could, they would really know themselves?"*

"Yeah."

Heck pondered the idea for a while before saying *"And share that knowledge with the grapevine of human opinion?"*

"Yeah, go public, so to speak." I pondered, then asked, "But tell me, Heck, would it make a difference in anyone's inter-personal relationships?" Well, I thought, maybe coming out from behind one's practiced daily facade might even boost one's degree of happiness, enhance contentment, make it easier to deal with emotional trauma, even overcome personal setbacks?"

Heck suggested, *"Such as death of a dear loved one, loss of a job, even a dramatic drop in the stock market."*

"Or make it even possible and easier for us to achieve higher goals in life?"

Heck acted distressed. Finally, he asked, *"But how can we find out about any man's true self? To begin with, let's take just one man."* He grew silent, then went on, *"Like I said, maybe, for starters, simply look at how the man is dressed. Perhaps you can tell a man by the hat he wears, or the shoes, or the coat...by categorizing his style, you know—"*

"Or by the car or truck he drives. Or by the whiskey he drinks. But, Heck, these are all overt trappings of his image, not a candid look into his true self. Sure, you can categorize a man, fill up the giant pegboard on the wall with characterization after trait, based on hat size, type of clothing—"

"Then what we will have is a cluttered pegboard with lots of irrelevant data pinned on top of even more irrelevant data." Whispering, Heck thought out, *"What if we follow only their hand movements."*

"What do you mean? You're changing the subject."

"Not at all. Do they dare touch one another, like the guy sitting next to them, other than to hand over or show a piece of paper, maybe a partnership agreement, a bona fide purchase order, or some document governed by the Uniform Commercial Code?"

I looked around the room, as much of it as I could see from where I was standing. I observed the actions of many of the men siting and expressing themselves at the round tables and nodded. "I see what you mean." I puzzled. "But their gestures are each unique to the man, to the conversation at hand, reflecting the emotions of the one speaking, like the gesticulations you might see in an Italian street scene."

Heck was getting more specific, *"Remember your conversation with the Reverend Marvin Wright, the chaplain of the old-line neo-conservatives. Just keep his little tidbit of advice in the back of your mind, Buddy Boy."*

I could feel Heck's hand on my knee. Then he laughed. I nodded. "And what else?"

Having tagged along with me, as was his usual behavior, Heck now really opened up, declaring, *"I'll tell you what else. These men are not going to alter themselves just for us in any way unless me and some of my imaginary friends—their own individual secret friends—subliminally suggest it to them. And then follow up with repeated urgings."* He paused, adding, *"Like repeatedly suggesting to them that this new display of personality is, Man, the new way to be and to act with the latest version of being cool."*

"Tell me how would you have them change?" I asked my secret companion. Querying him further, I asked, "What do you propose? Change from what to precisely what?" Puzzling for a moment, I went back to square one with Heck, asking why indeed they needed to change at all? What was wrong with them now, and what could improve them, that is, if they did indeed need improvement? What change in these men would Heck desire? In other words, what was there that might be revealed to us beyond what was plainly visible and what was presumably tucked away behind each of their streetscape façades?

Heck elaborated, *"It's our mission."*

"What do you mean, 'our mission?'"

Heck launched into what he believed to be and what he told me was the purpose statement of the IOIF, the International Order of Imaginary Friends. *"It is the mission of any imaginary friend to bring out the real person we are befriending, to allow him or her to be themselves, unencumbered by any of the hold-back leashes that restrain the true personalities and potentials of each of our human charges."*

"Very reassuring and inspiring," I acknowledged.

But Heck was adding an addendum, *"Well, you see, my friends and I believe that each man has his own imaginary friend."*

I had to think about that for a long moment, and then I confessed, "You know, for years, I thought I was the only one with a secret friend."

"You have been naïve, my friend."

"I always thought of myself as naïve in many matters. So, that is not news to me. Do you have another example of my naivete?"

Heck replied, *"Not now. We're talking about everyone's secret friend. That is, of the men who are here with us today."*

"Go ahead, you can reveal more, Heck. No one else will find out. There's just the two of in this conversation."

"Just you, really…but I will tell you the reasons most every human being enjoys the presence of their unique individual secret friend."

"Please."

Heck seemed to be organizing his thoughts. Before long he told me, *"You see, you humans are rather fragile people. Especially in the topsy-turvy personal development world that immediately follows the first year or so of your lives."*

"That's where parents come in," I suggested.

"No disagreement there," Heck assured me, adding, *"But parents are people, too."*

"No disagreement there." I assured Heck.

"Trouble rears its ugly head, however, in the nuts and bolts of daily life, for parents are not always there with help for the younger person suddenly faced with problems, perhaps even dilemmas, upsets for sure, where advice and back and forth musings may be needed in order for the individual to make sense of what is happening and to place it into perspective. These needs grow in significance as the young person grows older and is confronted with a medley of new horizons and new developments that, at first, may defy comforting explanations. Ergo, the need to bounce thoughts off of someone who is not threatening, not thinking retribution, and not planning to take advantage of our young

and vulnerable person. Hence, we secret friends come to the rescue. We're there 24/7, so to speak, not speaking literally of course, but in the young person's mind, to be called upon for backup, for answers, for ideas, for, yes, even creativity to wend one's way out of nasty situations."

"Geeze," I blurted. "What a diatribe."

"You disagree?"

"On the contrary. I agree completely. You've described experiences in life."

CHAPTER 11

Real Men?

———

Heck was saying, *"As to our situation at hand here in his massive convention hall, let's think some more about the minister Marvin Wright. His imaginary friend told me that he must continually remind Wright of his holy divinity degree, for carrying piggyback with it is his self-verifying sheepskin-bestowed authority to judge other people. That license is based on his training in the scriptures and his instilled belief in the ultimate judgment day. That is, and I'm sure he is so advised, so long as he doesn't impede the flow of money into his church from wealthy parishioners, of whom he must be ginger in his judgments."*

As I knew him to do, on special occasions, such as today, Heck continued, *"These men here with us today and tonight and for however long this goes are being what they are supposed to be, advertised to be, promoted to be, and thought to be by the other men, and felt to be by their wives and family members. But they are not acting the way they really are deep inside. It is there that their true selves lurk, caged there, stifled there, and hidden away behind the facades that conceal their true selfs."*

"You mean, they act as they are schooled to do so by those in charge of their religion. Accordingly, they become self-disciplined to conform to this dogma-designed image?"

Heck said, "*Yes, it is a learned and practiced trait. In actual practice, it may have been instilled in them by their secret friend to protect them from all the many and unexpected life's blows, enabling them to cover-up personal reverses, insults, losses at poker, poor scores on the links, embarrassments when you don't want to show your true emotions to other men and certainly not to a woman...or...and you can tell me—for we share our inner secrets, My Liege-- from your own inter-personal experiences.*"

I nodded my understanding. Of course, such knowledge in this day and age, if shared, might either benefit or maybe even hurt some folks. Or trigger a series of good or bad events. If, in society and during human behavior, a give-it-all-up and come clean rule book prevailed, it might be unwelcomed on life's daily stage. Clearly it would confuse people and could be a threat to the giving up a person's customary learned and trusted stability. Benchmarks of behavior, to use one of Dave's surveying terms, to which we are accustomed to observing in charting our course through life, would vanish. No one in the room participating in the conversation, or in anyone's presentation would know where their audience was at any given time. Fearing the results, fearing the embarrassment, fearing the truth, fearing the ramifications, fearing the destruction of image, fearing the loss of charisma from hidden attributes leaked to the press, fearing rebukes from superiors, fearing loss of one's reputation so diligently and carefully and cleverly branded in the competitive world of logos and images, fearing the loss of one's so-called "face," such an approach to life and its established behavioral patterns would mean confusion to life as we have come to learn it and to know it and to cherish it.

The change to full and complete personal inward disclosure would be as if the products on shelves in stores, in home improvement departments, in food departments were to suddenly disclose their true ingredients, along with the characteristics of each ingredient and how this particular product might affect, benefit, or impact, or hurt you—the purchasing consumer.

No, for sure I concluded, it would not work. Never. No one would come to the party. No one would play this cool new game. Almost immediately, everything would retreat back under the cover of regular old-style guarded conversation. We must keep the truth under wraps, hidden, disguised, incorrectly labelled, placed on the wrong library shelf.

Think what would happen to religious dogma, to law and legal proceedings, to prisons, to universities, to cultures, to propaganda. I mean, how many people would lose their jobs in devising their propaganda and feeding material into public relations pipelines? The same fallout for political campaigns, for charitable causes, for companies, their products and their management bigwigs, for people promoting themselves, for teaching the ivory towers of hidden ideas, would follow. I mean, suddenly Santa Claus would be exposed, the Easter Bunny would be run out of town, the time-trusted tooth-ferry and their coveted monetary deposit would disappear from under every child's pillow.

Traditional society would crumble, disintegrate in clouds of rubble and dust. On the other hand, advertising would become a cult of telling the truth. In other words, people would have to write product descriptions that alerted every consumer to the dangers, the possible misuse of the product, while at the same time extolling the product's presumed benefits. To myself, I added out loud, "Just think of the ramifications of developments like that."

"*Stop,*" Heck blurted. "*You're veering way off course once again.*" He acted a bit disgusted with me, and I suppose, as a result of his prodding, me with myself.

CHAPTER 12

Cars

———

Startling me, I felt a firm hand on my shoulder and an intense voice asking, "Is that your 10-year-old Chevy out there in the parking lot, Sir?"

I said it wasn't, but the voice then demanded, "What car or truck are you driving?"

I told him, "A stick-shift pickup truck."

In response, the voice, its hand still gripping my shoulder, advised, "Then I'll let you in on our special for this men's gathering here today—a brand new SUV of that make that will be a tailor-fit for you."

I reminded him I had just told him I was driving a pickup truck.

"Yes, but wouldn't you like to be the man telling all the other men here that you were successful enough to be driving one of our prestigious Dodge Ram roadsters." He pointed to the miniature silver automobile jewelry adorning his sports jacket.

I queried, "I didn't catch your name."

"Davey Dodge," he said.

I found it hard to believe him and I laughed.

He pulled his hand back from my shoulder, and looked at me in a haze of astonishment, asking, "What's so funny?"

"Your name."

"It's my real name, honest."

Heck said, *"Go for it."*

I did by telling him, "You see, in the very early days of automobiles, the Dodge Brothers were making cars."

"Dodge still is—that's the model my dealership sells," he proudly told me. "I'm the authorized dealer for this part of the Central Valley."

"Yes," I said, going on, "The proud Dodge Brothers put their name on the grill. Its chrome letters read, 'Dodge Brothers.'"

Davey looked at me querulously.

"You see, folks getting in the way of their cars thought the logo was telling pedestrians to get out of their way. That's when they dropped the 'Brothers,' part of the words on their cars' grills."

Davey said, "Oh, I see, their warning to pedestrians and other drivers to get out of their way." Then he allowed as how he didn't have a brother. And he turned toward other men nearby, readying his hand toward one of their shoulders.

* * *

Trying to make my escape from the friendly car dealer, I felt my surveyor friend Dave pulling me back into the large convention hall crammed with all the men. Dave guided me a few paces so I could meet, "The Warden of the local prison," who he introduced as "Henry Lockerbee." Dave promptly corrected himself and said, "It's not actually a prison, but rather a correctional institution."

Lockerbee nodded his approval of Dave's improved-upon name.

Without considering my question, I found myself asking, "Tell me, what are you correcting?"

Heck mumbled, *"Uh, oh!"*

I realized my mistake and wanted to retrieve my question.

Heck instructed me, *"You know, that to ask another male a direct question is a sign of your own weakness. I mean, you as a male, are supposed to know everything. A question, showing your lack of knowledge, gives the other male an invitation to put you down in the eyes of those who are listening. Or else, retort in a demeaning manner."*

"I know," I told Heck. "I thought I'd learned that in my male conversations."

"It's an axiom that we males have to re-learn over and over again. Now, we'll see how he handles your open-ended question."

Lockerbee, his strong and brutal male face looking straight at me, no, rather through me, was quick with these strong words for everyone around to hear, "What are you? Stupid?"

Dave didn't know what to say in my rescue, and so just stood there.

Trying to recover, I thought for a moment. Hearing no advice from my secret friend Heck, in a firm voice, I said, "I may not be that smart, but may I suggest to you that it is the inmates in your so-called correctional prison who are the dumb ones by having gotten themselves incarcerated inside your bailiwick in the first place." I paused and then I dared to stand there defying Lockerbee's stern judgmental look, and pose to the jailer a second question, "In your 'correctional' institution," and I dragged out my pronouncing his word, "what steps are you taking to correct the mistakes that got them there In the first place?"

As if on cue, Lockerbee retorted, "Put your hands behind your back for my steel handcuffs, and I'll personally usher you into the first of my many steps leading to your correction."

Heck spoke to me, *"Let's get out of here."*

My friend Dave was tugging at my arm to follow him else-where. I did, leaving Lockerbee, his handcuffs, his further prison steps, and the whole subject of his correctional institution. With re-lief, I cherished my rightful personal freedom.

CHAPTER 13

Well, Well

—

The next man I came up to and who gave me a deep smile was a younger man who promptly introduced himself as, "Peter Welch of Welch Wells."

"That's a tongue twister," I suggested.

"Second generation," he said, continuing with, "My father's been digging wells in this part of the Central Valley going way back to the 1030s. He…that is me now…are familiar with most of the unincorporated areas, actually all the way up into the foothills of the Sierra Nevada Mountains—I mean, really just about everywhere around here."

"I'd say, then, that you know the territory."

Peter nodded.

I asked, "But isn't it harder for you to find water these days?"

"Much harder," he acknowledged with a discouraging shake of his head. "The aquifer is dropping. In some places all we get is sand and maybe a trickle or two."

"I may be building a few houses here, probably outside the city limits."

"Then in all likelihood, you'll need to drill a well, perhaps a deep well, and that's where my firm will come in." He went on,

"But first you'll need a preliminary report from me saying that, if approved by the County Planning Commission, you will likely find water for your new homeowners below your parcel."

"And how likely is it that report will be positive?

Peter replied, "I'll need an exact location of your tract in order to look through our records to assess your location. Do you have a parcel in mind?"

Heck said, *"Be straight with Peter. You'll need his support."*

I advised Peter I'd be back in touch with him within a few days, and he said he'd look forward to working with me.

CHAPTER 14

Pursuing the Rumor

For many men, the acquisition of
wealth does not end their troubles.
It only changes them.

- Lucius Annaeus Seneca

———

I continued to wonder to myself and to Heck what sort of a world we would be living in if every man, at every instant, said what he truly felt or believed or wanted. Women, too. For example, take the Congressional aide and his confidential rumor, moments ago divulged to newspaperman Jim Early. What if the aide were to simply announce the rumor outright to everyone in the hall and watch while the dice rolled where they might? We'd all see what the die told us as to everyone's next move, and go from there. No cover-ups. Everything and everybody, all out in the open. What then?

But right away I set that speculation aside, for it was suddenly apparent to me that what was most significant at this moment was the nature and content of the rumor, and is it of any significance to any of us, or maybe even—if it was monumental—to all of us in the hall?

On that matter, Heck was quick to instruct, *"We must find out, for if the rumor has substance, it may affect us all."*

"I just said that."

"Yeah, I know. I'm simply underlining the importance of your thought."

I told myself, Heck knows something I don't. I asked, "You know—"

Heck nodded and told me, *"I know his secret friend."*

"And what does his secret friend tell you?"

"That's confidential."

"Look, Heck you're not his lawyer pleading confidential communication."

"The Aide's secret friend is claiming it."

"Tell me, how does your IOIF governing body, and I assume you must have one, resolve such dicey secret friend issues?"

"Bureaucratically, I'm afraid." Heck told me. Then he laughed.

"Forget it, then," I said.

"Forget it, then," was his mirrored agreement, to which he added, *"But let's do find out what is this rumor is, for I've a hunch, or better yet a sort of tip, that it is quite significant to everyone here. In other words, if true, it will have major repercussions."*

"You suggested you had a tip." With that from me, Heck suddenly disappeared, as he sometimes did, without warning, without a word. So, I decided I must find out for myself by seeking out the Congressional Aide somewhere in this mass of male humanity.

* * *

An almost empty bottle of beer in his hand, I found Randy Rhodes in serious conversation with Dave, my surveyor friend and event host, and another man whom I had not yet met. Seeing me come up, Dave introduced me, "Meet Don Davis, the largest general contractor in these parts."

Befitting his moniker, Davis was a large imposing man, perhaps created so as to be in keeping with the size and importance of his construction company, or so I surmised. Yet the big man was acting somewhat obsequious to the rather pencil-thin Rhodes. Maybe, I thought, it is that us folks, who are so far removed physically and every other manner of measurement from the nation's capital, are a bit in awe when someone from D.C. descends from the heavenly cloud of federal government and lands in the local neighborhood. Yet, after our handshake, Davis, displaying a detectable intent on his face, turned his attention back to Rhodes as he continued his conversation with the Congressional Aide. I heard Davis say, "Thank you for telling me this information in confidence, Mr. Rhodes—"

"—Call me Randy."

Davis began again, "Randy…you're talking about the need for a lot of housing units, plus tons of office space…yes, and retail, as well…that will be needed in our immediate Central Valley." Davis pressed the Congressional Aide, "Are you telling me I can, we can, count on this all happening? I mean you are describing some really big news. Yes sir!" Davis hesitated, "Your secret is safe with me. I won't tell anyone…I'll leave that up to you."

To myself, I didn't believe Davis' promise of his confidentiality. He's going to spread it like wildfire…although maybe not… maybe he keeps it, whatever is the news, to himself so that he can take advantage of the news by out-positioning himself ahead of all the other men here. So, what is this rumor, this news that Rhodes has just revealed to Davis? I had to find out.

Heck was back, agreeing with me.

The government man said to Davis, "Don, I want you to be up to speed on this so that you can be thinking of how to take advantage of the news when it is announced. I mean, you've been a big contributor in the past to my Congressman Schultz's political campaigns…."

"Yes…every two years…Randy, like clockwork. And each time our man has been re-elected by a landslide."

Randy patted Davis on the back and displayed a fleeting Washington, D.C. smile.

Davis said, "But Randy, even though it is you who are telling us about this, it does seem a bit far-fetched. I mean, to us locals… way out here in the hinterland. I mean, I know you are in the know back therein D.C."

"I am."

"Must be exciting…your work, I mean your mission, that is, your duties."

"Yes, it is. Thrilling. I'm serving my country and, of course, our beloved Congressman."

"You must get invited to the White House, too, I imagine."

"Yes, I've lost track of the number of times I've been to the Oval Office, actually."

Davis was so impressed that he almost dropped his beer, but Randy caught it for him at the last minute after my grasp missed. Dave laughed slightly, complementing Randy Rhodes on his manipulative hand skills. Then contractor Davis commented, "You know, Randy, that time you invited me to join you for dinner with party leader Jewell Nightingale and Congressman Shultz? Well, I was so enamored with her. She must be an effective political force in Washington."

Randy didn't comment, leaving Davis' impression to stand.

CHAPTER 15

Back, Years Earlier

———

In the older original section of the city, dating back even to the 1920s and actually earlier, to before World War I, water was free. There were no water meters in the entire city because there was an unending surplus of water. It was free for the asking and the taking. You could drink as much water as you liked, wash your car, water your lawn, nurture your garden and, if you had a bigger patch for crops, water the whole field with as much water as you liked. All free. No city or county meters to read and pay some government agency. No worries. Like Niagara Falls, water would always be flowing.

Back then, the few men running the city, those from the businesses that flourished at the time—plus the school principal, a church pastor and a priest, and of course the police chief, had gotten together and, in their camaraderie, had formed a private men's club. Only these founding brothers and their friends were admitted. In other words, the men who were running this part of the Central Valley could meet in private, talk, argue, drink, and decide solutions for their own issues and in time cash in on the opportunities. Shoulder to shoulder they could devise the projects and ideas that might well determine the fate of their lives and their families in the near future, even out into the distant future. In the process, they could and would shape the development and progress of their city and this part of the Great Central Valley of California.

They named their little private club "CVA," for Central Valley Advocates.

Later, as time marched on, they found themselves enmeshed in the nationwide presidential election of 1928. They each dutifully voted to re-elect President Herbert Hoover. With their solid block of votes, they endorsed his Republican Party platform and its doctrines of the day. In their collective male judgment, Hoover's words, deeds, and philosophy formed the fountainhead of civilization's up-to-date rules—the bulwark of humanity. Moreover, such thinking and philosophy was shaping mankind's civilized future, a future dedicated to those men of fortune who were in charge of society, those men (and the odd woman, maybe) who constituted the elite group of the "good" men of the world. Yes, for sure, they were the special persons who would see to it that reason would structure the code of government so that it could continue the good life for all men in the coming decade of the 1930's. There was to be no socialist or communist or other radical living in the White House who would destroy or imperil their cherished way of life.

Alas, they were sorely disappointed. On that "awful day" in November 1932, when the votes were being counted, they reacted in horror. To a man, they were sure the country was definitely on the brink of demise. For, in a landslide of votes across the country, Herbert Hoover had lost to New York Governor Franklin Roosevelt. To them, sadly, the basic tenets of Christianity and true and tested reason were now facing a deadly demise. The threats were obvious—for they were coming now, either from socialism or Godless communism. And which was worse? One or the other would soon become the rule of the land. These men, huddled in their CVA private club, vowed that they would henceforth unite their efforts, put to work their social and political prestige, along with their monetary resources to protect their property, their city, and their country from all of the anticipated dire fates.

* * *

Among the club rules to which a man was required to adhere in order to belong to this private club, the headline qualification was to support the tenets of Herbert Hoover's political party. The rule held forth each year onward from 1932, continuing through the elections that were to follow.

A club sticker was soon required on their vehicle's front windshield in order to trigger the wrought iron security gate on the gravel road leading to their club, housed in an old 1920's Craftsman style house. They employed every trick to keep out the riff-raff of seasonal farm workers and non-prominent locals. Their sacred slogan became "No Riff-Raff," which was promptly adopted as the club's secret handshake code of joining and of gaining entry into its sanctified confines. It was their way of defending the established social prominence of CVA members.

Meanwhile, as California grew and the Central Valley began to cultivate, grow, and ship its vast array of crops to the country and to the world, CVA men continued to support both their political group, along with their club's ideals.

As the Great Depression grew even more dire, had come the opportunity to buy an abandoned but historic tavern that set astride the original stage coach route that had led through the Central Valley, going north from Bakersfield to Sacramento and beyond.

At first, some of the men resisted the tavern's purchase, telling others that the building was derelict and they were throwing their money down a rat hole in a foolhardy purchase that would lead to wasting a lot of money. And then what would they have to show for having parted with their funds? To some, it would be a sin to foolishly spend the money that had come to represent the many paid memberships plus the profits from club events held over the years. These funds had been dutifully deposited in the bank, and then invested in time certificates of deposit earning a nice rate of interest, all of which represented the time-honored achievement of wise money management. As such, these reserves were available to them in the event of another depression, when it did come bringing with it a return to hard times. Everyone knew those certificates of deposit, now insured by the federal government, were both a virtuous asset and a mark of conservative philosophy keeping with age-old civilized money management principles.

However, by now the mood of some of the CVA members was changing, reflecting the group's evolving makeup and the influence of a younger viewpoint of younger club members mirroring an evolving society in general. At their Board meeting called to approve or turn down the stage coast tavern purchase, several of the newer members advocated for its purchase by imagining out loud what the club might accomplish by purchasing the old building. They told how they proposed to work to add to the prestige of the community by restoring the stagecoach stop and turning it into the larger building they now proposed to house their prestigious private CVA club.

One new member, John Waters, who had been proposed by several senior members to join CVA membership, was encouraged to stand up and advance his proposal. He did and, receiving the attention of all, delivered his argument for the future:

"My Fellow CVAers, please float along with me in my colorful idea balloon. It will soar into our future along an exciting path: Let us restore this historic building to its original stature as an important fixture in California history so that our children and their children can appreciate the heritage of our Great Central Valley, including the brave pioneers who, years ago, settled here from all over the world. As to our project, for guidance, we can call on restoration help from the National Park Service in Washington, D.C. where they are headquartered. After all, one of their primary missions, as mandated by Congress, is to preserve important buildings and sites across our great country and encourage restoration of the nation's patriarchy. Also, the head of the California State Preservation Office in Sacramento will lend a guiding hand in this endeavor. I propose that we work with a local architect with preservation experience, Pedro Mondragon, with whom I have already conferred.

"By pursuing this idea, gentlemen, we will bring about a building that will become the pride of our wives and children and all the folks in this part of the Central Valley. By adding an up-to-date dining hall in contemporary architecture to blend with the original pioneer style of the stage stop, we can host dinners and meetings, making our CVA and its new landmark a focal point of culture and activities in this part of the Central Valley. Our CVA cub will be the envy of all young men (and perhaps and surely this will come—welcoming young women—our daughters and granddaughters—as well."

Caught up in the idea, it must have been the enthusiasm of youth, the look in Water's eyes, and his vision of the future that took control of their meeting. It was an insight into their personal future, their CVA club's future, that sparked the vote in favor of the acquisition. Waters was resoundingly applauded in a standing ovation, and promptly voted to be in charge of their new project.

CHAPTER 16

Fast Forward to More Recent Times
Years Later, Yet a Few Years Ago

———

In a decade years ago, within the popular and intimate new private dining room of the CVA club, another eager younger man, Mark Shultz, was being hosted for lunch by two older members. On edge, as he felt his future political career was on the line, he was barely able to nibble at his sole almandine, while being careful not to sip too much of the Gallo Gewurztraminer in order to keep his wits alert to this day's important conversation.

The lead club member and host of the lunch addressed him once again, "Do tell us again, Mr…a…ah…, why do you want to represent our district way off there in the United States Congress?"

The younger man replied in as clear and concise voice as his training in and after school had taught him, "Gentlemen, our country is threatened by hordes of riff-raff who want to bleed our system of its resources in order to pay for their laziness by either not working or failing to form companies that will produce new products. I believe that we hard working men of this nation must protect what we have earned and what is ours to rightfully retain—what we have worked so hard to create for the benefit of our children and our grandchildren."

"Well said," from the two older men who greeted his remarks almost in duo, followed momentarily by, "The two of us are prepared—he turned to his companion and asked if he was going too far?"

"No, no, I'm with you, 'Coops'. Please go on with our young protégé here."

"Coops" continued, "So, 'Georgie Boy' here and I will back you with whatever funds are necessary to win your primary and general election. All we ask in return is that, through you, we can establish an information pipeline to Congress and the appropriate federal government agencies pertaining to their plans for our section of California. Such information will assure our continued connectivity with the opportunities to which we can take advantage in our always-ready cooperative effort with Congress that, in the process, will provide for both our community and our families." Taking another swig of his scotch, "Coops" said, "After all, young man this is our own little realm of California."

"Georgie Boy" added, "Has been, as you probably know, since way back in the mid-1800's."

The younger man was immediately ecstatic, as he pledged to his two hosts, "In respect and honor to the sacred heritage of each of you gentlemen, you have my sincere promise, Gentlemen, to move forward henceforth. Now, if you'll excuse me, it is time for me to go out into the district and canvas households and farms as I continue to line up my grassroots voters."

It was then, following soon after that promising lunch, that Mark Shultz hired another enthusiastic and even younger man, Randy Rhodes, as his Congressional Aide to serve in his office in the Capitol Building, as well as to head up his important Central Valley office. Shultz's local office was vital so that when elected to Congress he would be able to stay in daily touch with his Central Valley constituents.

Randy Rhodes jumped into his assignment, serving faithfully. He was instrumental in directing Mark Shultz's overwhelming election victory.

* * *

Shultz's political success continued with what was beginning to appear like assured subsequent reelections. Serving faithfully as his Aide, Randy Rhodes' juggernaut campaign rallies had continued successfully for five two-year terms for his boss. Shultz's efforts in the politics of Congress and within his political party had recently paid off in spades for him, with the Congressman having been appointed by his political party leader, Jewell Nightingale, who was from a district in Western North Carolina, to be the party's vice-chairman of the Congressional Ways and Means Committee. That committee, Jewell stressed to Shultz, oversaw the allocation of each of the federal purse strings. Shultz's new position awarded him with increased influence, both within his political party and across the nation's sprawling capital, among lobbyists, federal agencies, and the media, as well as back home in his district in the Central Valley.

In fact, this was not the first favor to be bestowed upon the Congressman by Jewell. On several occasions, she had traveled to the Central Valley to join with local supporters in campaigning for his reelection. Randy Rhodes recalled her visits and wished that, with her on his home turf, she would have been more supportive of his important position as Shultz's trusted Aide. But in reality, she had seemingly ignored him, or so he had come to feel, especially after Jewell's most recent visit when his apprehensions had been magnified during her stay. Given the private dinners the duo from Foggy Bottom had asked Randy to arrange during that shortened week of her stay, especially the one with the important general contractor,

Dan Davis. Randy had worked hard to try to please both his boss and Ms. Nightingale. Most of the dinners were with supporters such as Davis, but the rest, well…Randy wasn't sure, but for some of those dinners he had been left on his own.

Heck queried, *"Is there another dimension we're missing here?"*

I said, "Well, let's observe more and maybe we'll find out."

When general contractor Don Davis began today's query of Rhodes, it was, of course, with his prior knowledge of Rhodes' prominence in Washington as one of the longest serving Congressional aides on Capitol Hill. Davis surely believed, or so I concluded, that any rumor ignited by Rhodes had real fire behind it. I felt certain Davis believed such information was worth his personal attention and adamant pursuit.

When Heck reappeared, this was the same news reported to me in my secret friend's usual succinct manner, for which I thanked him. I then shared Heck's news with my surveyor friend Dave, who promptly nodded his concurrence, given its source, as to the rumor's weight and likely viability.

* * *

To my somewhat annoyance, Heck was now becoming painfully persistent, as he commanded, *"We must find out what is cooking with Randy Rhodes."* Heck was clearly defining the mission ahead for the two of us. He went on, *"Sometime this evening, or tonight, Buddy Boy, start probing all these guys for clues, for leads, for hints. You and I must find out! Scoop the rest of these guys who are not in the know."* He added, *"What fun! It'll be our little game to win."*

I agreed with Heck, as I realized the challenge for us was set. For sure, I now realized something quite important was cooking here in this convention hall. I told myself I've got to find out how, why, and when it is of major significance. I knew Heck was feeling the same way. But, what to do next? I supposed I could go right up to Rhodes and say, "Now, let's have it out, Mr. Congressional Aide. Government is supposed to be transparent. So, let's have the story told right here and now! What is this bloody rumor you are carrying around with you like some miniature A-Bomb about to be detonated?"

"No, too direct, too abrupt. He's likely to call security."

"Security? I haven't seen any…yet."

"Listen, they'll come out of the woodwork once they're buzzed into action. We're dealing with the Federal Government here. With them, Security is always on duty, ready and waiting, 24/7. Don't be naïve. Neither of us needs to be detained, arrested, held incognito without representation, without a chance to call for legal counsel, maybe forever, never to be heard from again. Just think of those poor guys at the prison in Cuba…whatsit called?"

"I've heard those guys in there get excellent medical care."

"Listen, you'll need it by the time they get through interrogating you. Especially once you tell them about me, your secret friend. Remember, I don't have security clearance for secrets at any level, you know."

"Okay, how then, Heck? How do you suggest we go about finding out the guts of this rumored-to-be important rumor?"

CHAPTER 17

When California Was Young

—

In the beginning of California as a state, for lack of some federal or state agency to do so, the newly-defined Yosemite National Park was administered by the U.S. Army, beginning with the end of World War I with the signing of the Treaty of Versailles and the boys coming home from Europe.

However, going back four earlier years to the summer of 1915, Americans, overloaded with all the dire news of the seemingly endless European war, both Easterners and Midwesterners sought relief from the all-consuming news of the endless going-nowhere European trench warfare with the accompanying deaths of so many soldiers, as well as civilians. For relief, the enticing lure of a change of scenery, combined with a sense of patriotism for their peace-loving country, folks who had heard about the Pan-Pacific Exposition in San Francisco sought a respite from the war news. Almost in unison, they exclaimed, "Let's go west to San Francisco...we'll drive our cars."

That there were few roads, the lack of motels (that hostelry idea not yet having been conceived), only a few scattered hotels and a smattering of old stage coach stops, proved no deterrent to their quest for something completely different to uplift their lives.

Americans by the hundreds rose to the challenge and invented car camping. They struggled with their cars and what roads there were enabling them to motor across the continent, albeit slowly, and eventually reach the by-now world-famous San Francisco Exposition.

Of course, the journey took longer than anyone had planned, but most made it all the way west to view the Exposition. Moreover, on their explorations, many also drove to see Yosemite, plus the giant Sequoia Trees, the mysterious and hypnotic expanse of the Pacific Ocean and, on their way, the Grand Canyon, the Pained Desert, the Petrified Forest, Native American reservations, prehistoric Anasazi ruins, the Delta of the Sacramento and San Joaquin Rivers and, of course, San Francisco Bay. Plus, there were the old wild west towns of Bisbee, Tombstone, the two Las Vegases—one in New Mexico and the other yet a tiny one in Nevada—and then there was Santa Fe, Taos, and the Sangre de Cristo and the Rocky Mountains to awe them with mountain majesty. As a result of all these people traveling all the way west to California, there developed a growing appreciation for the natural world of North America.

Meanwhile, former President Teddy Roosevelt had met the Le Conte Bothers, who later became the first back-to-back presidents of the University of California. They were singing "The Night They Drove Old Dixie Down" as they escaped from Columbia, South Carolina while the pillaging invading General Sherman's Union army burned everything in its way.

TR had also met the bearded John Muir, among others. All of these advocates were now clamoring for federal government protection of the natural wonders of the United States.

Within a few years, in desperation to protect and keep order, the U. S. Army was detailed to police the two wonderful and pristine Yosemite Valleys and, as well, protect the remaining Native Americans who called these valleys their home.

* * *

Trouble was, the U. S. Army was neither trained nor cut out to protect natural wonders, old buildings, legends, and especially indigenous Native Americans. Rather, they had been accustomed to shooting Indians.

Heck spoke up, a touch of admonition in his tone, *"Where are you going with all this background information? We have to tie it to all these men here in this big convention hall, don't we? Or am I completely off base?"*

As usual Heck was on base and I was the one who was off base, and subject to being tagged out by the first basement's glove, ball in grasp, having hit my exposed leg, or whatever was not touching the bag. So, I hastened to defend myself, "I was just thinking of some of the background of the American West."

"Can you tie it to the present moment?"

"No, but I do have a sense of its pertinence to this rumor of ours."

"Then share."

I tried, "Well, one of the men here in the hall, who is the Aide to the U.S. Congressman from this District, says he has a rumor, in which a number of the guys here appear to be quite interested, so I though it fitting for me to trace the story of the federal government's involvement in California and especially the Central Valley, inasmuch as the lands of today's Yosemite National Park begin at the eastern edge of our Valley."

"Okay, I guess, but it's a stretch, if I do say so."

"In that case, I'll try harder to satisfy you." In speculation, I said, "Suppose the rumor from this Congressional aide has to do with a development or change in the federal government's role in our

Central Valley? Perhaps the government's influence is to become a great deal larger economically."

"Or much less." Heck stopped and then commanded, *"Then, Good Buddy, you better find out what this rumor is all about."*

Good advice, I acknowledged to myself as I promptly set about to weave my way through the tables of men sitting and drinking beer and the groups of men standing and, like their friends sitting, negotiating business deals of some sort. My mind was now set on confronting the Congressional Aide, pin him to the wall, so to speak, and dissect this rumor of his. With Heck's urging and support, curiosity was taking control of me as I pressed onward through the crowds.

CHAPTER 18

The Man in a Wheel Chair

———

In my almost-blind rush, I spotted the Congressional Aide standing amidst a group of attentive guys over beyond a cluster of tables. Some were holding bottles of beer, some not. Failing to look down, I stumbled into a wheel chair and its handicapped occupant. As I quickly apologized to him, I saw that one of his legs was short, amputated, I presumed. I gushed, "I'm so sorry."

He nodded up at me, smiled, hoisted his beer bottle toward me, lowered it to his mouth, took a drink, smacked his lips in approval of the elixir, and replied, "Members of our IWO have an expression, 'We cherish apologies, for that's all some of us have left.'" And he guffawed.

"*IWO?*" from Heck. "*Let me tackle that acronym.*"

Wheelchair Man continued "You see, all people in wheelchairs know each other, and we have an international organization to advance and protect our interests."

Heck scoffed, "*Yeah, sure, and all redheads know each other. And all writers know each other. All dog owners know each other. All horsemen know each other, as well the horsewomen. Where does it stop?*"

"You started it with your IOIF."

"You got that all wrong. My organization was launched years ago, in fact, more than a century ago by this chap in London—"

Heck's revelation was cut off by a rousing cheer coming from somewhere across the hall from the direction where moments before I had seen the Congressional Aide talking to a group of men. I strained to see more of him along with the male group encircling him. Those with beer bottles, now had raised them in what I presumed was a toast, either to the Aide or to his surely just revealed rumor.

Heck urged, *"Get over there."*

But Wheelchair Man was grasping my arm with a vice-like grip, wanting to talk, I presumed. I leaned over, only to realize he had let loose of his wheels and grasped both my arms and, with all his might in his strengthened muscles, was pulling me down toward both him and his chair.

I could now get a more expansive view of the chair's advanced technology, at which I couldn't help but marvel. Not only was there a miniature television screen, but also a holder for his cell phone, coffee cup, a cell phone charging device, a GPS screen, and heaven knows what else. Had I the time and advanced curiosity, I might discover more of its cutting-edge features in a more thorough examination.

Distracting me, Heck was renewing his instruction to seek out the Congressional Aide. *"Get with our mission,"* he told me in no uncertain terms.

I managed to ask Wheelchair Man if he knew Congressional Aide Randy Rhodes.

"Yes, of course, he and Congressman Shultz have been effective advocates for my disabled brothers and sisters, back there in D.C., as well as here in the Central Valley.

"Let's go talk to him," I suggested, urging, I'll push."

"I can go under my own power. You follow," he advised, as he whipped around his chair, me in tow flying behind. In the process, he rang a warning bell on his chair to alert those clusters of males blocking his way so that he could make it through, as we headed, so I thought, toward the Aide, who I could see was still surrounded by those who had let out the rousing cheer a few minutes earlier.

CHAPTER 19

Restaurant Owner, Sam Matson

———

However, the developer who my surveyor friend Dave had mentioned earlier, Bobby Turner, the friend of Father Isadore who was going to try to buy the old abandoned K-Mart to make way for more church parking, stood in the way blocking the forward progress of our little wheelchair caravan. Aided by the helpful arms of a junior person, Bobby was unfurling a large development plot map of a shopping center presumably to be built somewhere nearby. Another man who wore a promotional nametag—unusual among the men here who seemed to know each other—that read "Sam Matson, Restaurant Entrepreneur – I'm Looking for New Locations."

Developer Bobby Turner was gesturing at one specific location in the rear of the shopping center, but he was promptly greeted by a profound "No!" from Matson, followed by, "I want my restaurant to be located next to the anchor, who you said would be one of the new regional Wal Marts. You know, tens of thousands of retail square feet selling everything under the sun, bringing everybody to the new center from miles around. Patrons will walk right past the front door of my new restaurant. I can display all my dinner specials, you know, and if they don't come in and eat that night, they'll remember to come back soon."

Heck quipped, "*Sautéed early bird – oh, yum – tonight's special.*"

"Enough," I told Heck as I tried, as did Wheelchair Man, to maneuver past the three with their shopping center site location map. But their roadblock with plot map spread wide was too formidable of an obstacle for us to circumnavigate. I ducked out from behind my new wheelchair friend and backpedaled until I could see what appeared to be a straight shot to reach the Aide, Randy Rhodes, toward whom I now forward pedaled.

I waved to him, which in turn earned a smile directed my way. Very politic, I thought. I asked myself what it would be like to build your entire career, shaping your family, your home—one in D.C. and one here in the Valley—while all the time having to act politic. You'd be at the constant and immediate call of your boss who, in turn, was at the call of his powerful national political party to which he was becoming a pivotal player. Furthermore, he was 24/7 duty bound to the district electorate who had repeatedly reelected his boss to Congress. In this assignment, the Congressional Aide was on continual call to orchestrate both the primary and the general election every two years—a clock work of excitement and career demands. As such, he was seemingly always raising money to defray the costs and expenses of television advertising, printing and distributing yard signs, designing and placing newspaper advertisements, designing and printing bumper stickers, plus flyers to hand out door-to-door, paying for lunches and dinners for constituents who might visit Washington and who expected to see and talk to their famous Congressman.

Think of all the money, all the time, all the thought, all the effort, and then, of course, what about your sartorial expression—be chick but not too cool, serious perhaps, yet playful, well sort-of, at least know which restaurant to take which voter to. Moreover, in your job on a daily basis, you were there to go back and forth with each of the many lobbyists. You had to tactfully know how to fend them off, yet at the same time how to take advantage of their knowledge of issues, discounting their biases, so that you were aware of their take on issues pertaining to their clients. Plus, there were the federal agencies you would be obliged to relate to, from whom you would constantly be getting information for your constituents, while promoting the businesses within your district back home, so that employment would go up and people would have jobs and vote for your Congressman in the next election. Whew! Wow! I was exhausted just thinking about what living that kind of life, with all its diverse pressures, would be like day in and day out, month after month, year after year.

Would such a life be fun? Would you make money? Would you be offered bribes, kick-backs, under the table envelopes heavy with currency, or letters of credit at a bank in D.C., or at home, or in Switzerland? Or diamonds and jewelry, or special 50-yardline seats at the Super Bowl, certainly the playoffs in some sport. But then, on the other hand, you'd be assigned to procure tickets to plays or musicals for your constituents when they came to town. Important people in your district who gave lots of campaign money for your respected Congressman's re-election, would be high on the priority list to acknowledge their requests. Also, there would be those people who wanted to meet important people in government, in the arts, in business, in whatever, wanting to arrange a lunch perhaps in order to show the folks back in hometown America how their trip went to the Nation's Capital and how they could swing meetings with important people by just touching the right number on their cell phones, which would ring at once in the office of the Congressional Aide.

And then, of course, there were the important constituents who were planning a trip abroad to some exotic foreign land and who pleaded for an introduction to the ambassador or the consul general in some far-off country. Just writing that letter on the Congressman's stationery would pave the way for a constituent to shake hands with our country's ambassador to the foreign land, or his assistant, while scoring points for your boss with opinion-leading voters in your District.

All these speculations formed a dizzying collage in my mind so that I was losing my footing and steadiness as I tried to navigate the men who continued to be in my way in my assignment to reach the place where I last saw Randy Rhodes.

All of a sudden, Heck warned, *"Look out ahead!"*

Sure enough, a policeman's uniform blocked my way. All I saw was the uniform until I looked upward to see a large man inside the uniform, which I quickly observed was complete with radio, weapon, night stick, handcuffs, not to mention the size of the officer wearing it. But the lawman was smiling at me, perhaps taking pity on his dominance of the immediate scene and my being so startled with his overbearing presence.

"Captain Bruno Smith," he said, addressing me with a smile, his hand outstretched, expecting a shake, to which gesture I immediately complied, as he told me, "I'm the Police Chief."

I returned his smile, asking, "Then you know Randy Rhodes, the Congressional—"

"—Of course, he's procuring more weapons for our department, actually plus an armored car…these days you never know…."

I gulped. "Are you expecting trouble of some sort?"

"No, but in my dealings with Washington, I've learned to take advantage of opportunities when you can, for tomorrow things may change."

"You mean elected political officials may change?"

"You got it."

"You expecting a change?"

"Not in this district certainly...Schultz and Rhodes—he pointed over his shoulder—have it, how should I say... sewed up tight...still, you never know." He added, "Talk to them, I mean Rhodes over there, and you'd think they're desperate for campaign funds...all of us give, you know."

Heck said, *"And they always win."*

I asked Police Captain Smith, "What do you think, Sir?"

"No one likes change, I always say, for change may bring revolution...thus our new armored vehicle. It's coming."

"Revolution or your new military vehicle?"

The Hulk stiffened. "Don't get cute with me, Mister."

"Or else?" and I laughed.

There was no replying laugh, or even an acknowledging chuckle from the uniformed and armed police captain, only a warning nod as I told myself that law and order will prevail.

Heck added, *"Most of the time."*

Quickly and with trepidation, I looked about but saw no red flags waving, no hastily scrawled signs of discontent, no signs of an uprising, no banners extolling a cause. In the tried-and-true American spirit, business as usual was ruling the day and into the evening. Be reassured, I told myself, American business represents stability and, maybe even more importantly, social continuance of established civilized protocols and accepted personal and group procedures, all of which serve as the protective bane of wanton change.

* * *

Comforted by my personal reassurance of life's major shields protecting against wanton disruptions in society, along with what I sensed was Heck's nod of concurrence, I saw that my host Dave was standing in front of me, smiling and waiting to introduce a casual-looking man standing next to him. This man wore a black western hat and a bright bolo tie around the collar of his cowboy-featured frontier-designed shirt. He had his arm around Dave's shoulder and was saying, "New events are my partner, Dave, for fresh news is what stimulates people to sell and buy houses, along with every type of real estate."

Smiling at me, Dave said, "Meet Pete Peterson, he's the leading real estate broker in this part of the Great Central Valley."

"Three offices to serve you," Pete said as he held up three fingers of his right hand. A friendly grin highlighted his clean-shaven face.

Pointing toward me, Dave said to Pete, "My friend here may be building some houses."

"Oh, good." Looking at me with his serious business mission in mind, Pete said, "He'll need expert marketing through a good broker."

I nodded for lack of knowing what to do. I finally managed, "I'll keep you in mind." Pete thrust his business card into my pocket for future reference. He responded by telling me he was born and raised in the Central Valley and knew every inch of it as well as understanding its people, especially their thoughts and ideas about land values, house designs, and values.

"For example," he began, "If you haven't built any houses in this area, then you need to know the basic floor plan that home buyers here want."

"Which is?" I inquired, always willing to learn something new.

Pete replied, "Folks here visit other folks by knocking on their kitchen door. Then you sit at their kitchen table and talk about this and that before you finally get to the purpose of our visit."

I asked, "But what about the front door of the house?"

"It's reserved for when a certain two people come to visit."

"And they are?"

"The minister and the insurance salesman. That's when you all go into the parlor. It's an extra room off the living room."

"When do you use the living room?"

"You don't. It's mostly for show. Or maybe where you and the missus might watch television or read the local newspaper."

I thanked Pete for his design insight. Indeed, this sort of floor plan was unique, I thought, to the Central Valley. I recalled, now that I had listened to Pete, I had seen such plans in some of the model homes I had recently visited.

* * *

Nudgingly, Heck was quick to remind me to get with my pursuit of Randy Rhodes. *"The rumor, remember, Buddy Boy! Find out what it is, and do it now!"*

Yes, yes, I said to myself and to Heck, as well. "Where is the Congressional Aide?" I said almost out loud. With all these men milling about, I can't see one particular person among them—Randy Rhodes. It was then I heard the music. An accordion, I told myself. While I've no talent in music, I thought I could at least recognize the music of such a distinct instrument. Who is playing, I asked myself and why now, all of a sudden? The tune was decidedly from yesteryear…ah, yes," I said out loud, "it's 'Happy Days Are Here Again.'"

Heck informed me, *"It's from FDR's 1932 political campaign. You know, 'A chicken in every pot', a rallying cry for voters who were starving from the dire effects of the Great Depression of the 1930's."* Heck then wanted to know, *"But where is our musician?"*

"I'm looking."

"Look harder!"

It wasn't that hard. Everyone could now see, standing by Randy Rhodes who had just vaulted himself up onto a tabletop, was a man wearing a Greek-style hat holding his polished and shiny red and silver accordion. His body swaying with the melody, he was producing sweet and memorable music, while he voiced the overriding words of FDR's 1932 presidential campaign song.

In a moment, the happy, smiling musician concluded the song and then, with everyone's eyes upon him, his voice carrying across the convention hall like a clarion call to rally troops to join a popular cause, perhaps a crusade to save the world from evil, he said, "Randy here has an announcement, which will be of interest, I assure you, to everyone here in this hall this evening."

"The rumor. He's going to tell us." Heck announced, and I nodded in anticipation.

In reaction, pandemonium reigned across the hall as everyone was now talking to the person next to him as they speculated on the forthcoming message from Randy Rhodes. It took a while for the Congressional Aide to calm the rampant speculation with the volume of concurrent male chatter. Minutes later, but maybe it took as much as ten minutes for the last of the chit-chat to subside, Randy Rhodes patted his accordion player on the back, looked around the room, hoping for and expecting attention. He began by saying loudly, "My friends, I have some important news that I'm sure you will all be interested in—"

Suddenly a brass horn blurted a loud long note that didn't want to stop. The musician in charge of the horn seemed to have an endless supply of wind energy to blow into the instrument. Of course, the overriding horn promptly diverted attention away from Randy Rhodes, who was poised to deliver his important information to the men gathered around his table and throughout the hall. Simultaneously and en masse, everyone in the hall turned from watching Rhodes to visually scanning the hall to see who was the horn musician abruptly competing with the Congressional Aide. Moreover, why was the horn blower so rudely interrupting the Aide to Congressman Shultz, who was on the verge of voicing his valley-shaking announcement.

In angry reaction to the interruption, loud and derisive rumbling male comments of protest filled the oversize room.

As the horn continued, yelling along with accompanying sounds of a scuffle were heard coming from yet another section of the hall. In the midst of this uncontrollable disruptive commotion, a forceful young male voice shouted vehemently, "You will all see it, for it is coming—soon, maybe now! My generation will lead the anti-capitalist revolution! We will soon—" But his words were lost in the shouts of older male voices in a cacophony of protest against what surely must be a revolutionary viral millennial or Gen X generational manifesto. Maybe it was a voice from an even younger generation. To the men, however, it was all coming from irresponsible youth. Yet, at least two other young male voices promptly joined in, as if on cue and in unison echoing the first man's cry. Their voices sounded like a trumpeter's clarion call, which was now emanating from yet another likely young dissident musician.

A police whistle blew loudly. There was an ensuing milli-second of silence as the attempt from the law-and-order uniformed police captain whom I had just met was intended to restore order. But the soon exhausted whistle blast didn't calm the room. More shouts of protest came from other younger voices, as competing older voices shouted, calling for eviction of the disturbing youths. Cacophonies of horns blaring along with older male shouts dominated the cavernous convention hall.

The unruly commotion now replaced everyone's sense of propriety. For the moment, noise from horns and shouting voices had interrupted most men's desire to hear the important announcement from the Congressional Aide. Randy Rhodes had come all the way from Washington D.C. prepared to make his momentous announcement at this all-day and all-night men's event deep in the heart of the Great Central Valley of California.

CHAPTER 20

Six Young Women Having Prepared for the Day

———

During their first year as students at the area's popular community college, six young women, who had known each other in their respective Title IX high school sports programs, vowed to continue their friendships. They met often to pursue what they had come to deem as the dedicated political mission of their maturing lives. They were of varying ethnicity and sexual preference, but united in what they saw as their mission—what they believed their higher education was preparing them to diligently pursue.

For weeks stretching into months, they had been working together to compose their youthful manifesto with its dear-to-their-hearts objective, which called for: A) Exposing unwanted male verbal and physical abuses, B) Extolling women all over the world to join forces to save the planet from the approaching ravages of Climate Change, and C) Either reform or do away with Capitalism in favor of what they had decided to label as "Common Good Economics for all sexes and all genders." It had taken them a series of emotionally-charged meetings to hone their message to the point where they felt embolden enough to be ready on this particular day to join their horn-blowing supportive male cohorts in staging their disruption of the all-male convention. They neither cared nor knew that the meeting in progress was about to culminate in the announcement from Randy Rhodes.

If they had a leader among their ranks—and none of them would acknowledge that they did have such a person—it would likely have been 20-something Stefania. She was the enthusiast who regularly called the time and place of their meetings and made certain the coast was clear so that the other girls could secretly file into the college's political science department's private coffee room after hours on Friday nights. That was when most students and faculty, too, went to either the movies or to populate one of the Central Valley's proper and acceptable dance halls.

In composing their resultant manifesto, they had taken turns composing and editing. To its terms and demands, at the last minute they had added a call for free community college education, together with forgiveness of oppressive student loans for their older brothers and sisters. Reciting what they had considered recent oppressive events, the wording for their declaration was set forth in straightforward language. In its prologue, it stated that colleges across the country had given up on receiving additional federal college operating and research grants. They blamed this curtailment of fundraising on the federal government's business-oriented austerity philosophy which had been arbitrarily imposed on restricting funds for working class families.

In addition, they wrote that, needing to find another source of money to pay for growing college bureaucracies, colleges everywhere had embarked on publicity programs that encouraged students to borrow money to pay for their tuition and living expenses in the form of federally insured student loans. The newly minted loans, with increasingly larger amounts of debt money, were actually designed to inject operating money into the colleges, rather than really paying for their education. It was, they said, taking the form of student-paid tuition. it was, so their argument went, that students were financing American education, instead of what had been the other way around—back in yesteryear when community colleges paid for student education through forms of taxation of real property in community college districts. Indeed, they argued, in the process, Capitalism had run amok to the detriment of the people, especially younger Americans, who were saddled with expensive and unwieldy loans, which in reality were financing the operating expenses of each college.

Satisfied their statement was in its final form in order to meet their time deadline for this particular afternoon, they had convened incognito around the corner of the Central Valley convention hall. They were disguised in male outfits, their blonde, red, and black hair tucked neatly under their railroad engineer caps, each of which they had sewn in a slogan, "Women will not be railroaded into supporting the evils of Capitalism."

In fact, on their own artfully designed letterhead, they had printed several hundred copies of their manifesto. Across the top of the title page appeared their photographs, showing each as a serious determined-looking young woman intent on her mission. Their attire varied from a sartorial message of combativeness to one of sexuality. One young woman carried a toy pistol which she pointed at their own camerawoman who was snapping the photograph of the six women in the melee.

As they circulated among the men in the crowded hall, they handed out their manifesto and explained loudly, "We are women saving our Precious Mother Earth Planet!" If queried by any man, they might reply, "We will replace Capitalism with a plan that benefits peoples of all ages and all genders."

I knew Heck was reading one of their flyers. I waited for his take, but from him there was only silence, and I worried.

Now, with gusto and with unhesitant steps, the young women continued to circulate among the mostly older men handing out copies of their platform to those male hands who would accept the multi-colored document. At the top they had depicted three genders of sexual orientation hugging each other in a bond of camaraderie under the caption, "We are human beings entitled to equal treatment by Congress, and as well by each of you men."

As they maneuvered, the girls had allowed their hair to escape from its confines and swish back and forth with each of their female steps, so that the men realized they were, in fact, being confronted by a group of young women. That triggered many of the older males to call out in dismay, "Someone let a bunch of girls in here." Followed by, "Where's our police captain? We can't have all these women in here. This gathering is for men only."

CHAPTER 21

Dollar Signs Twinkling Like a Meteor Shower

We can easily forgive a child who is afraid of the dark;
The real tragedy of life is when men are afraid of the light.

- Plato

———

In typical male behavior in what was quickly discerned as a crisis situation affecting all sentient beings, an alert few of the men instinctively sensed the surprise and clearly unwelcome circumstance that had arisen. As if a higher authority was calling upon them to act individually, they rallied to their immediate male assignment, which they perceived was to get control of what they deemed to be a rising male challenge. Their actions would surely and promptly curtail the commotion and turmoil, rendering the situation under control, and restoring expected calm.

So, they accepted the challenge of the moment with the same aplomb as if a five-star general's personal trumpeter had blown a "charge" blast on his military horn. The particularly-summoned men rose to the occasion as if leaping forward across the trenches of warfare and onto the battle scene. One after the one, in sequence, the little group of men addressed the six girls in a friendly and condescending tone with a variety of commanding words, such as, "Honey…my child…darlin'…cutie pie, what are you doing here? Aren't you cutting class?"

Hearing the condescending words of one male, Coach Lou Parnell called to him and said, "Look, Dude, this young woman was one of my star female athletes in our high school last year; believe me, from her athletic performance, I can assure you she's no darlin' to you!"

My surveyor friend Dave, verbally tackled another male as I chimed in with yet my own reprimand, suggesting the guy solicit opinions from the protesting girl, not a put-down of her being active in pursuing her cause.

Heck supported me with, *"Bravo!"*

I heard the sexist minister instructively call out, "Let us pray."

Suddenly coming from a street outside the hall, loud sirens blasted.

Another man, hearing the sirens, suggested, "Our brave police captain is coming to our rescue by calling out the riot squad."

Dave said, "Our police department doesn't have a riot squad yet. There's been no need to recruit and pay for all those shields, guns, and armored vehicles."

"That is, until now," one man retorted. The sirens grew nearer and louder, their blare ricocheting from wall to wall and ceiling to floor around the hall like a battery of aberrant bullets fired at random.

Heck worried, querying me, *"Are we safe?"*

"Stay close," I said.

"I always am," came Heck's reply. *"Duty bound, remember?"*

* * *

In response to the sirens and moving with alacrity, Stefania made the athletic leap upward to stand at the side of Randy Rhodes on the tabletop. Grabbing the microphone from him, she commanded in a fierce female voice, "Girls, go out the back door—and I mean now!"

The dissident male musicians, horns in hand, quickly assembled and followed the girls as the lot of young protesters, in rapid unison, made their exit. Their quick movements enabled them to avoid the incoming police crew, weapons drawn, who were entering the hall through the double-entry glass doors from the opposite direction.

Continuing to grasp the microphone with both hands, Stefania's brilliant nail color flashed excitement to the room as if she wore imbedded jewels. Set to leave the hall by delivering a stern message, she shouted into the microphone, "The young people of this country want equal rights, equal respect, and equal opportunities in today's America. You men here in this hall can help us achieve this very basic goal. What is so complex, so socialist, so communist about our goal? The answer is 'nothing.' Our goals are simply for basic humanism."

With that, Stefania reversed her calisthenics display and made her downward leap to the convention hall floor, turning promptly to rush out the back door. She was followed by two male policemen, who were abruptly restrained by Coach Parnell and my surveyor friend Dave, a duo I joined as backup, as Coach Parnell told the officers, "These young American patriots have staged a sincere protest here today. Let them go in peace."

CHAPTER 22

Our Historically Successful System of Capitalism. What's So Wrong, if Anything, with it?

Time destroys the speculation of men, but it confirms nature.

\- Marcus Tullius Cicero

———

Watching Stefania follow the other girls out the back door of the big hall, I did something I am not accustomed to doing. That is, I made a snap decision to follow them out the door and try to learn more about their points of view. After all, I was learning about the men here and now. To balance the gender scale, I felt the desire to see the world and maybe even our own Central Valley society through the eyes of these young women.

Outside the hall, on a sort of dock where trucks might unload products or special background stage sets for events, and standing next to a wooden shed built to conceal dumpsters and large refuse cans, I saw Stefania. I hailed her with what I intended and felt was a friendly call. Approaching closer to her, I explained that I'd left the hall wanting to learn more about her views. I asked, "Can you explain to me what is so wrong with the Capitalist system we live with today in this country?"

Stefania looked at me with a combination of dislike, distrust, and disdain.

I waited for her to begin.

I sensed Heck's curiosity equaled mine, as he observed, *"Balls in her court."*

Stefania came up to me, all the way, in her few steps, looking me in the eye. She pushed the decorated nail of her right hand's index finger into the folds of my white shirt and said, "You're one of them, aren't you?" She waited a feminine moment of my silence and then told me, "I mean, you benefit from all their business dealings, don't you? You know them all, you are let into their little and their big business deals." She paused and said, "But, you know, you older men don't dream like we do, we girls, we students. We've our whole lives ahead of us as soon as we graduate. We're looking for careers, maybe marriage and a family, but mostly we want to participate—participate in the action, the benefits, the perks—you know what I mean? We each want to feel like this society is for all of us, not just you men. After all, you men—I mean, from your private club in town—run things for the benefit of each of you, not for the benefit of the rest of us, especially us girls and our female friends. Don't you get it? We want to be part of society, feel like this is our land, as well as your land. That's our dream! Do you get it?"

Stefania had hit the ball hard, and I was having to duck her return.

Then she further challenged me, "I'm sure as a man, you've dreamed the American Dream. That dream is not a gender-specific all-male night adventure like one of your wet dreams. We girls dream the American Dream, too. Trouble is, when we do experience that natural excitement, it is always interrupted with the same nightmare, over and over again. In that scary interruption to our female American Dream comes an interruption of flashing electric billboards, each one proclaiming that we—because we are women—do not qualify for the culmination of the dream with our success in the business world. To the contrary, we are each put down and herded into a room full of flowers and babies and washing machines and cook stoves and dresses and beauty salons and beauty products to satisfy the good-old and age-old American Capitalist consumption and profit rules. Ever go into a department store?"

I nodded. Of course, I had many times.

"The first floor is all about beauty products, and I mean there are counter after counter brimming with the latest and most expensive products from—well, you know the endless list of products from skin oils and…shit, it's the entire fucking first floor of the damned department store. That's the scene we girls face when we dare to dream the American dream and project this sacred fantasy of our careers and our dreamed-of success in today's world." She waited a brief minute, and punctuated her remarks with, "In your view, we're in the beauty category, not the brain category."

I recalled my department store visits and could only agree with Stefania's critique. I had to walk up or take the escalator to the second floor to look for men's clothing and shaving needs.

Stefania had paused for a moment, but then, with a new thought bursting for expression, so I felt, she said, "Woman is the life and birth of society. Men must respect woman, for woman can bring vital life to your society, when all you men want to do is fight among yourselves." She added, as if an asterisk to our conversation, "Just remember, my friend"—she said that word with ridicule, I thought, concluding with, "Woman is your real hope for your future!"

With that diatribe addendum, Stefania gave me an expressive finger. Immediately she turned away, but then turned back and in a penetrating tone advised, "The system…your system…is broken.

You can either fix it or replace it." She laughed a cruel laugh and called loudly, "Replace it, I say!"

Her lesson, in her mind, having been delivered, she moved away from me to join her girls who were each clapping and smiling at her, as they, together, left both the outdoor scene and me. Watching them go, I decided to return to the interior of the convention hall, for what, I knew not.

Heck commented, *"Whew…I'm speechless."*

CHAPTER 23

What Now?

———

Back inside the big hall, trying to get my thinking straight follow-ing my mindboggling experience of being confronted by Stefania, I tried to tune in and focus on what Randy Rhodes was saying. I was in time to get in on the end of his kneejerk response to the young peoples' demonstrative interruptions to the events. He was now pos-ing his question of the moment into the microphone, "Again, can any of you tell me what is so wrong with our historic system of Capital-ism? After all, it's been in place for how long? I say, we've followed it diligently for some 250 years. We began with the seminal American Revolution that instilled free enterprise and democratic Capitalism in the thirteen Colonies. Our system has lived on thereafter through today." The Congressional Aide voiced his question and comment in a mixture of surprise and an ideological rallying cry, as he hoped for an answer from the men below him and around the hall who were close enough to hear his dismay. His statement supporting Capital-ism was met with cheers.

His demeanor now switched to inquisitive rather than didac-tic, as he reacted to the young peoples' protest of moments ago, their distributed flyers, and their musical horns that had interrupted him making his grand announcement of the day.

Randy was relishing his center-stage position, augmented by all the lights, all the eyes, and all the ears being focused on him. I suspected that he'd never enjoyed such a enter-court spotlight in his life—not even when he was called upon by his Congressman to deliver a set of facts to the President of the United States in the most important of all venues anywhere—the White House's Oval Office. He had once thought he could never top that experience. Now he was doing so.

Only moments ago, he was about to reveal his earthshaking announcement to the men gathered before him. It was the announcement of most importance to all of them that he had prepared, having performed in solitude several rehearsals of his delivery. Yes, it was his most important time. He deemed it a valley-shaking announcement to the male voters in his beloved District. His words would become a headline highlight to add to his precious career scrapbook entitled "Randy Rhodes' Events." All that was only moments ago when the interrupting demonstration had deprived him of that exciting and ego-building memorable feeling. Now, he yearned to dial back his life and the attention of the men—dial it all back in time a few moments ago to that momentous event, that elixir feeling he had so treasured. Yet he was finding it difficult to do so, having listened to the profound words from the girls, and then Stefania's leap up beside him when she had grabbed the microphone of the day from out of his hands in order to broadcast her remarks.

However, looking around, Randy saw standing among the group closest to him two members of the city's nearby exclusive CVA men's club. One, "Coops," nodded at Randy and repeated loud enough for him to hear the local men's club's forever slogan, "No riff-raff! Keep them out!"

"Riff-raff" is surely a non-sexist, non-gender term, Randy reasoned, so he nodded an anticipated agreement toward his, and his Congressman's, long-time supporter.

I could sense Heck's fists close and then open, only to close again.

"No," I told my secret friend. "Let it go."

"*I can't,*" Heck protested and went on, somewhat out of control, I thought, "*Look, in your research of American history, you've filled your mind with a lot of the intellectual and factual forces that have made this country a beacon of human rights shining around the world. Is that not so?*"

"Yes," I said. "But this is a civilized gathering of Central Valley businessmen, not an intellectual symposium."

"*And women, too,*" Heck amended, continuing, "*In that case, Buddy Boy, let's get to Rhodes' rumor or, should I say, his important announcement that he was about to tell us about right before the music and the pretty girls interrupted him with their call to arms.*"

"Not that, Heck. They were simply exercising their rights as Americans to express their ideas and themselves. After all, they are human beings."

"*Okay, the rumor. Or should I label it his announcement? Query him…and I mean for you to do it now!*"

CHAPTER 24

The Awaited Announcement from the Congressional Aide

—

As he had had to do many times during Congressional Campaigns and during his visits to the White House, Randy Rhodes relied upon the rapid recovery skills he had honed over the years. Now, regrouping his mental faculties, he began his announcement, first calling for quiet in the great hall. It took a few minutes of waiting for conversations to simmer down. He held aloft his microphone and turned from side to side to get the attention of the clusters of men gathered around the table on which he stood. From beneath him, they looked up in full attention and anticipation, awaiting his important words.

Randy Rhodes began, "So, my friends, in comment upon the disturbances, let me ask you: what is wrong with Capitalism? For 250-some years it has brought us an exciting democratic nation, public education, medical benefits, international corporations providing jobs to millions and millions of people, not only in America but across most of the world.

"Let's go back in time to when our forefathers and mothers came to the New World. What did they see from their sailing ships as they were about to disembark onto land after six weeks or more of being tossed and turned on the open seas? What did they envision?

What did they plan for? And then, after they landed, what did they bring about for themselves and for their descendants?

"I'll sketch it for you, if you will allow yourselves to go back to those days long ago and try to see the world through their eyes and in their imaginative minds. They saw a vast new continent with opportunities for all—their shipmates and the hordes of shipmates to come to the New World in each of the ensuing years. They envisioned an environment open to new ideas, new types of government, freedom of religion, and freedom of expression—not bound by the aberrant wishes of a thousand-miles-away, an ever so distant, geographically and mentally, British monarch, who viewed himself as an all-powerful ruler who had been designated by God to be in charge of that country and the New World, as well.

"This new land was not to be restricted in enterprise and profits by greedy businessmen in far-away London or Glasgow. Instead, these pioneers saw opportunity for themselves and for others of like mind. They saw their own fortunes awaiting them. But they knew if they invested capital and applied their hard work, the results would bring happiness for their families, including education for their children. That's what the opportunities of Capitalism in the New world offered these early pioneers."

Heck whispered, *"What about the girls, Randy? The girls?"*

Randy was going on, "Sure, some folks may have fallen by the wayside. That's better than almost everyone falling by the wayside under communism, dictatorships, and monarchies, as has happened in Russia, over and over, and in China and other countries around the world."

Randy paused and reflected, "Those girls we just heard from need to know that had we not had a Capitalist system in this country they might not have had a house to grow up in, and might instead be camping out in makeshift tents in some remote desert, with no schools and no future to look forward to, and no hope for a decent and happy life ahead.

"Capitalism is a system that works for most people. Let us not allow the few who can't get with the program to disrupt our livelihoods and close off our future lives and the futures of our children and grandchildren."

Standing tall and projecting his voice loud and clear, the Congressional Aide concluded with, "Gentlemen, and also to the girls outside if they are listening to me, I say let Capitalism reign over America, over the entire world."

I voiced an audible "Bravo," joining with so many others with matching expressions from all the men who were now looking up in admiration at Randy Rhodes.

Heck said, *"Not so fast there, Mr. Federal Government. Cut to the chase, please."*

Randy was going on, "Capitalism with all its benefits and profits, is now what I'm about to offer you with my announcement— to you, my friends here in our Congressional District."

Hoots of support for the esteemed Congressional Aide as the men waited to hear the gist of the announcement.

Heck said, *"Now hear this!"*

"I'm listening," I reassured Heck.

* * *

Randy Rhodes began with, "Ever since California began—"

"—1850," called out a man in the back.

"Yes, thank you," Randy acknowledged and smiled, continuing, "Ever since then, water has been the real true gold of our state. But now, 170 some years later, water is running out. We've drained the aquifer beneath us until many of our wells are pumping air and sand—dry as a bone. The land surface has sunk as the water table below drops farther and farther into the earth. In other words, dirt is now filling the void where water once was plentiful. Yes, water was there waiting for the taking, waiting to be pumped up to the surface. In searching for water today, wells have gone deeper and deeper and deeper until they could still only pump sand. Most of the water that has been available to us in the past has by now been expended to water our precious crops and maintain our vitally important agricultural fields here on the surface."

Randy waited as he visually took in a great many of the men listening and nodding their understanding. He went on, "Now we have new laws just passed by our State Legislature intended to regulate water, our water. This law is called the Sustainable Groundwater Management Act—or Sigma for short."

"Repeal it!" several men shouted in rage.

Randy explained for those that didn't know, "It's your own California Legislature. Remember, I'm back in Washington with the U. S. Congress and our beloved Congressman Shultz."

"Yeah, yeah, Randy, we all know that."

Randy smiled. "Just to be clear."

"We're crystal clear," several said in confirmation of the civics point. Marston Wright, the high school civics teacher nodded, as another man appended, "Gin-clear."

Randy went on, "As I know our friend Pete Peterson here, an important real estate broker, will confirm, the value of agricultural land is no longer going up in price. Uncertainties have come to dog values due to each parcel's questionable access to water, the great resource we all took for granted until recently. As you know, each of you being supporters of business here in the Central Valley, investors, prospective ranchers, and other buyers of real estate don't like uncertainty in their lives any more than the rest of us."

Randy waited as the sea of faces peered up at him from around the room, ready for his next words, which followed, "Now I can tell you how this may play out. And that's where our beloved Capitalism comes into your lives, and where each of you here today and tonight may well benefit."

Randy relished in the undivided attention he was receiving. All those ever-so-many eyes focusing upon him made him feel good all over. Their smiles, their stares, their anticipations for his next words, all bolstering his expanding ego, served to enhance his self-importance. The scene was confirming his opinion of himself as an important person in Washington, as well as here at home in the Central Valley. His parents would have been proud of him here today. His wife, well, his former wife, too, if she had simply—was that too much to have asked of her? If she had just stuck with him instead of…well, that was another drama. Randy quickly suppressed those thoughts and returned to address his waiting and, he was convinced, admiring male audience.

In a voice mixed with excitement and anticipation, Randy now told the men, "Here's the news," Randy paused as if searching his mind and appended, "Well, I can't for sure confirm it…yet because, you know the procedure, the Appropriations Committee in Congress has to vote necessary funds, but Congressman Shultz and I feel certain it's all going to happen, and happen soon."

"What is?" asked a man right in the front standing beneath Randy.

I heard Heck asking the same question.

Randy waited for seconds to pass, seconds that would assure the continuing rapt attention of the male entrepreneurs and civic leaders filling the convention hall. "Here's the deal, my friends. A large Federal Agency is going to leave the confines of the encircling Washington Beltway and relocate out here, right into our Great Central Valley."

Quite obviously, it took a long moment of silence for the news, or maybe it was only the rumor, to sink in. During the instant quick, ensuing back-to-back moments of comments from the men, such as, "What did he mean? Did he mean that? Is he fooling with us? Is he serious? My God, if he is serious, just think what that means for all of us here, getting in on the inside track…. This is the opportunity of a lifetime for us."

I thought of the early pioneers coming to this far-away continent. As their sailing ships sighted their seemingly never-ending land of opportunity, they told themselves, "I am certain that on these virgin lands our fortune awaits us, here and now, ripe for our taking."

Heck was recalling Randy's history-driven words as he ruminated on what he thought was one of the reasons for the American Revolution, *"And the profits will belong to us, and not be going off to those greedy guys back in Glasgow and London."*

Automatically, I nodded and felt that, as usual, Heck was right on.

Then, to no surprise, for maybe they had each heard Heck's observation—although not likely—came the reactive conversational buzz.

Suddenly, you couldn't hear yourself think. Instead, you could only hear the men around you commenting in uncontrollable excitement and enthusiasm. Each reacted as they instinctively visualized themselves, armed with this hot new tip about the future, their future, they were jumping onto the opportunity. I was sure they were thinking about the influx of new residents moving here from Washington, D. C. and its suburbs, bringing with them a burgeoning demand for housing. In addition, there would be an accompanying need for commercial office space, plus new retail stores, new big box outlets, new schools to be built, new hospitals to be needed, new everything to be added to the new streetscapes of their town and countryside here in this section of the Great Central Valley.

My surveyor friend Dave tugged at my arm and said, "You are my first customer. Find me that point of beginning so I can start the survey for you!"

Marston Wright exclaimed, "More classrooms, more students, more minorities, more to do. Challenges for each of us… wow!"

Father Isadore exclaimed, "Thank the Lord. This means we're going to have to build another church—this one with ample paved off-street parking for our multitudes of new parishioners. I must call my archbishop immediately with the news. Glory be, soon there will be a lot more money coming into our diocese."

Real Estate broker Pete Peterson told a friend, "I'm going to need to hire more sales people…yes, and probably open three or four more offices. Just think of the commissions coming in from the sale of land, and from all these new residents purchasing newly built homes. It'll be a built-in real estate bonanza for my firm. I'm going to get the jump on it and corner the market for raw land in this part of the Central Valley!"

I thought of the housing I could build, given the right financing from my new friend, bank manager Volk. I could rush out now and tie up several good locations. I, too, readily joined the convention hall euphoria suddenly ruling the moment.

From nearby, I heard Dr. Singer exclaim, "This means a new hospital, hiring more nurses, more incoming patients, more satellite clinics…more pill sales." And he laughed uproariously.

At this moment, heard above the uproar of men's plans for their perceived futures, came Randy Rhodes' voice, "You may ask me which federal agency I'm telling you about, and my answer is—"

"—Many in the audience interrupted the speaker with their

own off-the-top ideas of which agency it might be that was planning to move its headquarters from the Nation's Capital to the local region of the Central Valley. With so many agencies being cited—and the local men knew many of them, but far from all—their citation of names proved to be an acknowledgment of the vast size of the federal government of the United States—a size, as they listened to the many guesses voiced by the men, some told themselves, was commensurate with the vastness of the convention hall in which the name guessing was now under way.

The acronyms of the multitude of federal agencies, as the men thought more about the federal government, were bubbling up from the convention hall like bubbles rising from boiling water in an overheated caldron.

Hearing some of the men's diverse thoughts, Randy shouted, "No, no, my friends, let me explain...no need for you to guess. I'll tell you which agency it is."

"I know," shouted one man. "I just heard about this little-known agency that buys vehicles for the post office and other federal departments. They need a race track for testing each model, and I just remembered there's that old abandoned stock car race track out east of town in the foothills of the Sierras."

Another shouted, "Randy, isn't it that agency that tabulates something or other? You know which one I mean?"

One guy said, "Yeah, Randy I know who my friend there means. I'll think of it in a minute."

The growing laundry list of agency names, some real, some imaginary, some made up on the spot, filled the minds and voices of the men in the hall. Yet few men were fully briefed as to the actual long arm and the world-wide reach of the federal government.

Heck commented, *"No one of us here today really knows. Let's let the Aide tell us, for Pete's sake."*

For the moment, I set aside my dreams of building and selling a lot of houses, counting the profits therefrom, to agree with Heck.

It was Pete Peterson, in fact, who spoke up. Somehow, he had come upon a microphone-speaker built in to a box in a wall, there to be plucked and used for routine fire drills, into which he now commanded, "My friends, no, no, it is one specific agency that I am certain we all know."

That set off another wild round of speculation, which ranged from agencies, such as the Internal Revenue Service to the Armored Corps of the U. S. Army. "Tanks will love training in our foothills," one man advised his friends to their nods of agreement. He went on, "I recall my training in tanks at Fort Knox. The terrain here is similar." Another, agreeing, told how he had fought "the Commies" while serving in the tank corps in Viet Nam.

He got prompt applause from nearby military veterans.

Randy said, "Thank you for your service." More applause.

Heck said, *"I'll bet Randy had a deferment."*

I thought, calculating in my mind, and suggested, "He's too young. The draft was over when he was eligible."

"Let's hear it for our nation's youth!" That, again, from Heck.

Randy Rhodes was now showing his impatience at revealing his secret of the decade. He said to a dude smiling up at him, "Why don't they shut up and let me tell them who it is?"

The friend said, "Maybe they'd rather play the guessing game than really know. But maybe they think your news is really pie in the sky, Mr. Rhodes."

In his knee-jerk negative reaction, Randy held back his frustration tinged with anger at the man's dissent, suggesting to him almost automatically, "Please call me Randy."

The man replied, "Then, Randy, take this microphone-speaker and tell us all which federal agency is going to relocate from Washington right here to our Central Valley."

Overhearing, Pete Peterson rushed the microphone-speaker to him. The man handed it up to Randy Rhodes who grasped it and immediately shouted into the mouthpiece, "Let me tell you guys. Now!" Reluctantly, but with anticipation, the Aide waited. Slowly the room quieted. Almost in unison, the eager heads turned up toward Randy Rhodes, the important and popular Congressional Aide to Congressman Mark Shultz. Still standing table-top, and in response to the men's urgings, Randy spoke in a clear modulated voice, "It is the National Park Service."

"I just knew it," came one man's voice. Didn't I tell you?" No one around him nodded, as he went on, "They have an office in Tucson that selects the books to be sold in all the national parks and monuments—they'll move that here, too, like I said."

Several around him looked at the man askance, but then, quickly digesting the news themselves, joined in. Excitement was now the common denominator, the dominating popular subject, the inspiration to the men who were populating the convention hall.

Every man here, well, almost every man, but also indirectly, including the ministers, the heads of non-profits, the law enforcement officers—most, but not all, were figuring in their minds, making projections into their future—how they each were going to advance their careers, their pocketbooks, their prestige in this unexpected and earthshaking community development. They fashioned themselves, their companies, their organizations, and their talents, coming together as pioneers in a new and virgin land. Yes, they were on the verge of making and/or enhancing their personal fortunes—for the benefit of themselves, their families, and even for their grandchildren's children. Yes, it was a time of ebullience, a time for their brightening futures, a time for expectations, a time for wild happiness, a time they wanted to share with their business cohorts, their families, especially their wives, their sweethearts, had they one, which some did.

Several, however, were having an opposite reaction. Standing nearby, Tod Ryan, who I had overheard from conversations owned a small shoe store. He looked at me and, his face dour, said, "That means I'll need to expand my store—double its size—and hire more clerks and ramp up my inventory, and, you know, I don't want to do that. I'm happy with the way things are now. I sell maybe a few shoes a day, and go home, and I'm happy. My one clerk is like a family member. He's been with me for years…."

Another businessman echoed Tod's viewpoint, telling me, "I left LA to get away from the rush, the pollution, and the noise so that I could come here to run my little coin laundry. I've just the right number of washers and dryers. I collect the coins every evening, go to the bank with my night deposit bag and go home to my wife, dinner, and relax. I don't want to double my size and start hiring people. I will hate going back to being responsible for having employees."

* * *

Charley Counts watched the announcement and the ensuing cheers unfold before his eyes and ears. Slowly he came to realize that here today was the opening into the community he needed in order to establish himself and his franchise for making and selling colorful signs—signs on trucks, cars, lawns, buildings, any kind of sign, for that's what his national franchise gave him the exclusive technology to design, to produce, and to sell.

Standing within reach of Pete Peterson, the real estate developer, Charley suddenly saw his opportunity open up before his very eyes. Immediately he approached Pete, his arm outstretched, one of his franchisee business cards in hand, which he thrust into Pete's hand as he said, "Mr. Peterson I'm your real estate for sale sign man for all your properties, your houses, your new buildings. I can place your signs all over the Central Valley announcing to the whole world that you are the person to call for all their real estate needs."

By now I was standing next to Charley and was the second recipient of receiving his business card, for which I nodded acknowledgement. I heard Charley tell Pete, "Prices you won't believe, Sir. I do the work with my advanced high-tech sign-making equipment my franchise organization has imported from the Czech Republic."

Pete raised his eyebrows, smiled and tucked Charley's card in his shirt pocket, advising him that the two of them would soon be in touch for a long lunch to plan their strategy.

CHAPTER 25

Truth Be Told

———

Observing the prominent real estate broker and the eager sign man shaking hands, I sensed it was a time for me to pause and re-assess this presumably earth-shaking, or should I label it this valley-shaking development? As I reviewed the facts as stated by Randy Rhodes in his announcement, I came up with several elements that troubled me. First, I thought more about the news and the manner in which it had been delivered. Sure, I wanted it to be true, for it was a harbinger of money to be made, maybe a lot of money by a lot of the men here today, and likely at least a little bit by myself. If it were true, I would hasten to tie up one or more parcels of land, design a street layout, apply for either city or county approval, depending on city and county borders, design the houses, try to get construction financing, and then build and hope to sell a large number of new homes. At least, with most house sales, or so I projected, I would net ten to fifteen percent of the sales price per house—that meant making good money, for that was what this gathering of all these men was intended to foster—no apologies, for here was American Capitalism at work. Money and making money had become so important in our lives, in our plans, in our values, along with family, of course. But it takes money to raise a family and provide for them.

Momentarily I diverged in my speculating to query myself: what are my innermost values? What is it that drives my true self to get up in the morning and go to work, to conceive new ideas, and do the things I do in order to either express myself and provide for myself and to make it possible for members of my family to thrive and be happy? I thought how, if called upon to jump up on the table and stand beside Rady Rhodes, what might I say to this group of men today to justify myself. It would be my enthusiasm for pursuing a project—in my case to build homes—in order to further our society and provide places for some of the incoming hordes from Washington, D. C. to live and enjoy their jobs and their new lives here in the Great Central Valley.

Randy Rhodes was justifying himself, for sure, with his announcement. I could tell right away from his self-satisfying demeanor that he was on a high, having made his important announcement to elicit the thrills of the men gathered around him. With his news, he was changing the lives of families, changing the lives of a battery of federal employees in Washington, Virginia and Maryland and all the suburbs surrounding the nation's capital. As well as the lives of those people who were dedicated to running each of the many national parks and monuments, plus there were the effects upon the many related supply contractors serving the National Park Service.

However, pausing, my mind parsed the announcement that Randy had delivered. I reviewed the reactions I had watched as the men jumped up and down so excitedly on hearing the news. To put it all into perspective, I wanted to write down the words of Randy's announcement on my computer keyboard and then print out the result and go off in a corner and read what I had written and think about it, analyze it, and critique it. After all, one cannot simply pursue an interim episode in their lives with only one simple bit of information.

I mean, where were the media rumor mills that surely must

be and have been circulating prior to Randy's announcement? I had read nothing in the newspapers or seen any comments on television. That was not so unusual, given the size of the federal government and the number of media stories being followed every day. Of course, a fresh set of rumors was being generated each day in this busy and complex country.

I was beginning to wonder what Heck was thinking, but then I knew right away as I heard him comment, *"Buddy Boy of mine, consider these two critiques of our Congressional Aide and his announcement."*

"Go on," I urged my secret friend.

Heck did, beginning with, *"Number one, doesn't it strike you as peculiar that such an announcement about an agency of the federal government, especially such an important agency that everybody in the country knows and admires because of all the national parks and monuments, would not come from the Congressman himself, rather than being leaked out to our local population through his Aide?"*

At once, I thought Heck's point quite valid and said so to him, adding, "Yes, with Mr. Early, our local newspaper and television man being in the audience, ready and able to feed the story out to our local and the nationwide media outlets, plus, of course, his own local TV station, KROP. I can read the headlines now and visualize the commentators on TV on the evening news and across tomorrow's headlines. It's going to kick off a massive response, plus comments, pro and con, I should think, from citizens of this section of the Central Valley. I know not what the sum total of peoples' reaction will be—in fact, here's several ideas: 'Just think of the traffic and the overcrowding of our schools when all these people move here from Washington. We're not prepared for such an economic gusher. Each of our lives will be upset in ways we can't even imagine. I don't want such an intrusion on my life. Let all those government employees stay back in Washington. After all, government people think differently from the rest of us folks. Besides, the traffic from all these cars and trucks will become unbearable—all those cars and delivery trucks, and all that construction for new homes and commercial shops—why, our community is going to be disrupted in the worst way. Our churches will be overwhelmed, and those Easterners will bring all sorts of liberal ideas into our conservative homes and our kids' schools. I vote no. Go back East, mister federal government. Go back to where you belong.'"

Heck nodded, and went on, *"Now, think a little deeper, which I know you can. On another subject."*

"I'll try, but about what?"

"Water."

"Why water?" I asked.

Heck didn't reply, leaving it for me to explore the topic. I recalled what the Central Valley well man, Rich Welch, who I had met earlier, had told me about wells being dry, pumping up only air and sand. And then I remembered Randy Rhodes telling us about this new legislation passed by the State Legislature in Sacramento, setting rigid regulations as to who can drill wells and who can't. This new law meant there would be fewer wells because there was less and less natural water in the aquifer for us to tap into. I said to myself, "Well, if that's the case, then where is all the water going to come from to enable us to build more homes and more commercial buildings, all of which will need water? If there is no water, there will be no approvals from the county-wide zoning agencies, and no approvals from the city regulators if a new development was to be located within city limits. Did Randy Rhodes and his Congressman have answers for these questions before they made, or rather before Randy made his announcement, presumably with the blessing of his Congressman? Had they thought it through? Had the federal agency—The National

Park Service—also thought it through? I mean, surely, they must have done so, for otherwise they are blowing bubbles from a pipe that's soon going to run out of soap, or whatever it is you put into your pipe in order to blow bubbles. Was this whole episode a futile exercise in fantasy? And, if so, what was Randy Rhodes motivation in making the announcement in the first place? Surely, he's not gone off his rocker, or has he, given my observations? That is, if I'm right on, but maybe I'm not. Maybe it's just all very innocent on his part. Yes, for sure he must have got caught up in his own idea, ranking it as a 'go,' and moving forward, bolstered by the rapt and attentive support he sensed from most all of the men here. Poor Randy must have been overcome with an overwhelming onrush of enthusiasm, somehow uncontrollable.

But then, think of the media. The news is going to be all over the media in no time at all. Surely Randy knows that and realizes what a range of reactions he is likely to get from leaking the story in the advance of announcements from his Congressman or the federal agency itself. So, what is really going on here? I wanted Heck to weigh in on my dilemma.

It was then that I saw Peter Welch, my new well-drilling acquaintance. I waved at him and each of us maneuvered through the crowds of men so that he and I might talk. I could now pose my vital water question directly to him for answers, as he was the expert on water, at least its existence, and in what quantities, and clearly in which locations relating to the aquifer.

Heck urged, *"Yes, you must ask him about the water question right now. Let's get Randy's weird story analyzed by an expert."*

I wasted no time in asking, "Peter, what do you make of this stupendous revelation?"

"Well, my friend, in view of the new state laws restricting well drilling in the Central Valley, to me, Randy raises the immediate question of where is the water going to come from to supply all the new real estate developments that will be needed, given the relocation of this huge federal agency and its employees from Washington all the way across the continent to our area." He added, "As we each know, without a reasonable guarantee of water, you can't get development approval from either a city or a county anywhere in the Central Valley."

Heck nudged me, *"Then what's the answer?"*

I asked Peter that very question.

Several men around us, overhearing our conversation, were drawing close, eager to hear Peter's response.

He said, "In our world today there is a finite quantity of potable water. Sure, there are the saltwater oceans, and a lot of rivers, many polluted with toxic water. That means, good water is a precious commodity. It's like gold and silver and platinum and all the scarce rare earths."

The group now forming around Peter and me nodded in unison. Eyebrows raised, we each waited, hoping Peter would clarify. Instead, he pondered the matter, leaving us each trying to guess, or out-guess his next remarks.

In our brief acquaintance, I had not regarded Peter as an especially scientific-type person. Drilling holes in the ground wasn't necessarily rocket science, yet on the other hand it wasn't an elementary endeavor either. One had to know the geology layers below the Earth's surface plus, in this day and age, be adept at performing ground penetrating radar with the new technologies available for geologists, archaeologists, geothermal scientists and other academics, not to mention those oilmen whose job it is to test for possible hidden fields, even at great depths. At least, that was the scope of my understanding of what lay beneath the earth's surface and how to find out about it. Peter was no simple man with a large sharp shovel. Today he had to be more man than that—a lot more.

My laudatory assessment of him was promptly borne out as he said, "Standing here, fellows, I've been speculating on some rather fringe ideas that I've been researching and inquiring about with my geology friends at our local state college."

"Please go on, Peter," I implored. The other men around nodded, most moving in closer to our now-tight circle so they wouldn't miss a word from our knowledgeable water man.

He continued, "To date, only a few have really looked into the location of artesian water flows coming our way from the Sierra Nevada or even from lower in altitude in the foothills. That's a huge area— spread over mile after mile." He pointed east toward the mountains and the foothills and then continued, "Until now, there's been no need to explore up there, other than for the occasional mountain cabin home. Over the years, as you know, we've simply tapped into or dammed up the rivers flowing down from the Sierra Nevada Mountains."

The men around him each nodded in agreement.

"Those rivers and the reservoirs behind the dams became an adequate source of our water down here at lower levels in the valley. If we hadn't done that, all we'd have had is the seemingly endless aquifer, available simply for the drilling down. But now, with old wells going dry and new wells not finding water, we have to deal with this new state law that Randy Rhodes has reminded us about. As he told us, and a fact that most of us were becoming aware of under this new law, we can dig only so many new wells and only in certain places. And only so deep.

"A few days ago, my geology academic friend, Dr. Harlan Rockford and I had lunch in the fancy dining room of the exclusive men's CVA club in town. He's a new member and wanted to try out their cuisine. The club is reaching out, among other places, to the college for new members, trying to stay up to what's going on in the world around them, as Dr. Rockford explained to me.

One of the men, showing his impatience with Peter, interrupted and pressed, "Peter, surely without water, and I mean large quantities of water, all these new houses and commercial buildings will never get planning commission approval or a go-ahead from the regulating state water agencies. After all, those guys in Sacramento have the power to approve or disapprove new subdivisions anywhere in the state, so I've been told."

Peter nodded.

I asked, "So, what did the professor have to say during your lunch?" Several men echoed my query, as did Heck, who quipped, *"This well driller guy should have been an academic, for he can't seem to get to the nuts and bolts of the situation."*

I told Heck he was being too critical, too quickly, but I shouldn't have taken that tack, for Heck's feelings were the last I wanted to offend.

I heard Peter going on, "Well, Dr. Rockford told me about some Internet research he had been conducting on water. You know, you can find out a lot on the Internet. Why, a friend of mine who was working on his wife's application to join the Daughters of the American Revolution was missing one important link for her to prove her ancestor's role in the Revolution. You know, in your application to the DAR, you have to have written proof of your lineage—not just, oh, my grandmother told me, or I heard it from one of my cousins. Well, wouldn't you know it, he googled the question and right away a link came up with the documentation he needed to complete her membership application."

Heck observed, *"That's nice, but where were we?"*

"Patience," I urged.

Seeing my raised eyebrows, Peter got back to the topic at hand, "Well, Dr. Rockford told me about an article he'd picked up off the Internet by simply googling his question having to do with locations of artesian wells, and in addition, flowing artesian water sources. What came up, he said, was a most unexpected reference to a newspaper story dating back to 1858. That's right, 1858. It was from a small newspaper printed in Sacramento."

"What'd the paper tell you?" I was eager to know, as were the others.

"It was most strange," Peter allowed, "for the article told of a deep, deep well that apparently had been hand dug—well obviously, for they didn't have back then the kind of high-powered drilling equipment we do today. Anyway, that centuries old well finally hit a fast-flowing stream of water, an artesian flow most likely. In fact, the article said it was really an underground river, and it was conveying lots of fresh water down to our Central Valley, presumably from somewhere deep in the Sierra Nevada Mountains, all the way to the east of Sacramento."

"What did that tell you?" asked one of the men.

Peter was quick to reply, "That there are likely many untapped sources of water in the foothills of the vast California mountain range running north and south all along the Nevada boundary, that is, if we'd just get our equipment up there and search."

Excited murmurs ensued.

"But wait, there's more," Peter said softly, and the murmurs quickly subsided as all eyes and ears focused on my well-digging friend.

"Back in the dining room and sitting at the table next to us were 'Coops'—that's his nickname, and everyone calls him that, so I learned—he's the head man of the private men's club. Sitting across the table from him that day was our popular Congressional aide, Randy Rhodes."

A series of disparate comments came from all of us. I said, "Go on, Peter."

"That was when I overheard 'Coops' telling Randy about how he and a few of the men in the club had banded together to take options to buy a package of land parcels located in the Sierra Nevada foothills east of here."

Every one of us commented eagerly to each other.

I said, "So, Randy and 'Coops' both know about these artesian flows and the water we may be able to access that will give us sufficient flow to get approvals on all the developments necessary to provide for the many new houses and buildings needed to accommodate the large federal agency in Washington that wants to relocate here with all its employees."

"Several men agreed. Peter did, too.

"But where?" I asked, repeating, "Where do we drill? I mean where do you drill?"

"Well, I think it's obvious. We go to the county courthouse and find out where the parcels are that 'Coops' and his friends have taken options on." He went on, "After lunch, Dr. Rockford had offered several clues. "But he advised me that his thoughts were confidential."

Yet, I sensed that Peter knew where these parcels were located. And if he knew, then the Congressman must have known, as well, as a result of his Aide's lunch with 'Coops.'"

Heck commented, *"Never have the prospect of so few holes dug in the dirt meant so much to so many."*

CHAPTER 26

Inside Information

———

My surveyor friend Dave, who had invited me to this gathering, was my next contact. I soon found him seated at a table toward the back of the hall drinking a beer with a man who I quickly learned was the judge of a local court. Dave introduced him as "His Honor James Burns." They had been friends, so Dave explained, for quite some time, and Dave hastened to tell me that he had known Jim when he was a lawyer in town—that was before he was elected to the bench. Dave told me when that happened, he had asked Jim's wife how he should address him being a newly elected and respected judge. She had replied that to her he was still "Honey." She told me I could use that greeting. I laughed, but Dave told me he still called him Jim.

"Jim and I were just discussing the potential liability of the developers of a sprawling office building outside of town." Having been a real estate developer most of my adult life, I was interested in stories relating to any aspect of the business. So, I listened as Dave and Jim went on to discuss the building, the location of which was familiar to me.

"Sits on the hill overlooking Highway 33 coming into town," I said to their prompt agreement and asked, "So, what's the problem?"

Judge Jim said, "Actually the building lies astride two hills, and it's collapsing in the middle."

"No soils test to get building approvals?" I asked.

Dave said, "Oh, yes, two as a matter of fact. Both showed stable soil underneath each end of the building. With that, the County approved construction."

Automatically, I queried, "So, what happened to the middle of the building?"

His Honor replied, "I said there were two hills, not one. Unbeknownst to the soils engineer, the county building department, or anyone else today, there was a draw from an old creek down the middle. That's where the building is caving in. Only last week, we found out from vintage city maps that that this forgotten draw, back in the late 1920s, was the site of a large Hooverville, you know, those out of the way locations where unemployed homeless men gathered cardboard, metal and anything they could find to craft one ramshackle house after another for themselves."

"Yes, Dave added, their shacks were made with whatever material they could scrounge. Everyone hereabouts had forgotten about the Hooverville, for that was almost 100 years ago. Meanwhile, the draw had filled in with refuse and dirt, and the soil, had it been tested, would have obviously shown to be quite unstable."

"So, who is liable for the damages?" I asked Judge Jim.

He said, "Well, I suspect several lawsuits will soon be argued by attorneys in my courtroom."

"Pity the soils engineer," I suggested.

"And the surveyor," Dave added.

"And the architect" the judge added.

"Perhaps even the contractor," I speculated.

"And the real estate broker," I heard my friend Pete Peterson comment as he came up. "I know the story well. "We sold the site to the developer. And they persuaded a group of investors to ante up their money to own the building when it was completed."

"Uh, Oh," came from Heck, who added, *"Color my remark in spades!"*

I opened a beer, sipped, and posed the obvious question to the group, "Tell me, why am I in such a risky business?"

Heck reassured me by explaining, *"Because, Buddy Boy, you thrive on the challenges. More importantly, I am supporting you."*

I expressed my heartfelt thanks to my secret friend.

"Part of our IOIF Code of Ethics." Heck added, *"But right now, I'm thirsty. Let's get back to the subject of water."*

I sat down at the table with Dave, Peter, and Judge Jim. Each of us had our bottle of beer and were sipping. I looked at each of in turn and slowly asked, "Please tell me what you make of Randy Rhodes' announcement, and Peter, more about your account of the lunch you had with Dr. Rockford at the CVA club and what you overheard from the conversation between the academic and Randy."

Dave briefly filled in the judge, who of course had been in the hall when Randy made his announcement.

The Judge said, "Sounds as if there's a bit of collusion going on." He thought for a moment and said, "What do we really know about this guy 'Coops?' I've met him but don't know about his background."

Dave began to fill us in on what he knew, "As a surveyor wanting to know as much as possible about a tract of land so that I get all the dimensions right, here's what I know from my investigations. His family goes way back, and I mean way back. 'Coops' is short for Coopersmith. He's considered by some to be the main character in an exclusive group of associates and friends. In this group, the men and even the wives, are each known by uncommon nicknames."

Judge Jim urged, "Go on, Dave."

"Here's what I understand. 'Coops' ancestors were soldiers who trekked across the vast expanses of North America with General Kearney's Amy of the West that invaded Alta California and raised the stars and stripes above the Customs House in Monterey, the former Mexican seat of government. After the Mexican War was over with the signing of the Treaty of Guadalupe-Hidalgo, as you will each recall, California soon became a state. 'Coop's ancestors had been soldiers in General Kearney's Army. After their discharge, this close-knit group of fighting men that had buddied up on their trek across the west, became enamored with the opportunities they saw in this newly conquered land. They conferred and decided to remain in California to seek their fortunes."

Dave continued, "Next, I must tell you about this experience I had a few weeks ago in the CVA club. I was having drinks with a developer client, when I observed 'Coops' and 'Georgie Boy' sitting on the other side of the walnut paneled library drinking. After my client left, I stayed on to read some local area reports I had discovered on the library shelves. That's when the two men, by then well-oiled, staggered out of the club.

"At that point, the head steward, to whom I had given a nice tip for his attentive service, came up to me. I could see he was interested in talking. His name tag read Ramon. I encouraged him, and he told me he and his wife Luna had recently become citizens after having been here a number of years from Mexico.

"Following my congratulations, he gestured toward the leather wingback chair where 'Coops' had been sitting and asked if I knew about 'that man's' family background. I said I didn't. I sensed he didn't particularly like 'Coops' for one reason or another. Ramon then told me had been disturbed to have overheard a conversation between 'Coops' and another member, who he knew was a banker.

Ramon said, "I could tell they were talking about Mexican

Land Grants in California. I listened carefully for 'Coops' was explaining that a number of the grants were derelict in the required process of acceptance. He said he was citing the Congressional rules set up by Congress in, yes, it was back in 1849, required, he said, to gain their legitimacy."

Dave then disclosed to the rest of us at the table that he had done some background research on Mexican Land Grants. He reported, "Most made it to acceptance, so I understand from a history student at the local college who has studied the matter for her master's thesis. She told me that most of the lands in California, Arizona, New Mexico, and Texas were covered by Mexican land grants. The political and military leaders in Mexico City were handing them out right and left to their friends up to and even while the Mexican War was raging.

"From her, I learned that her legal research into court records revealed 'Coops' ancestors had banded together in what they called "The Circle" to contest several land grant approvals, if indeed the Hispanic heirs had even gotten approvals, because the paperwork had to be in English, not Spanish. The Circle became very powerful as they won several court decisions governing three large land grants. In the process of gaining their legal success, they assembled huge tracts of grazing land for sheep, goats, and cattle. Then oil was discovered down near Bakersfield.

"She told how The Circle made out like the robber barons they had become. Circle members became rich and powerful. That's one reason for their being able to assemble the land for the private men's club in town. And its rehabilitation. As well, their funding the campaign coffers of Congressman Shultz ever since. Even today, no one in town dares challenge them. This part of the Central Valley is their playground, so to speak."

"In other words, these artesian water flows may be on their lands?" I asked.

"Pretty much that way," Dave answered.

Peter said, "Yes, I think that could be right."

I suggested, "This means, my friends, that the new houses and commercial buildings that will be needed for the federal agency and its many employees will most likely have to be built on lands now owned by these members of The Circle, who, so I have heard, call themselves 'Franklinites.' For, on their lands is where there is apparently sufficient water to get all the many building approvals necessary."

I continued, "That means, everyone else, including me, will be left with tracts of dead dirt, unable to do anything with it other than lay out soccer fields and baseball diamonds by donating the land, or having it taken by eminent domain by the city and/or the county."

They each nodded.

Impatient to know, Heck asked, *"Why the name Franklinites?"*

Being also curious, I echoed the query to Dave, who explained, "'Coops' and also many of his friend's ancestors were natives of an area in Eastern Tennessee, whose leaders, right after the American Revolution, formed the 14th state, naming it Franklin. Residents and backers of the idea became known as Franklinites. However, the new state was short-lived, not having been recognized by the newly-formed U. S. Congress. Within a few years, the handful of counties that constituted the state called Franklin were incorporated into the new state of Tennessee."

Dave felt obliged to add one more bit of relevant history, along with his opinion, "Residents of this area of the Appalachian Mountains are fiercely independent. When the Civil War came, they voted to stay in the Union. Even today they vote differently than the rest of the state. Those traits seem to have come down through time to 'Coops' and his business pals."

Judge Jim observed, "It sounds as if they are treating this section of our Central Valley as if it were their own separate state, and they are the legislature, the courts, and the executive branch."

CHAPTER 27

Business Deals

———

Looking around the large hall, I could see from the body language and the intense looks on the men's faces that that the earlier more light-hearted conversations had changed into serious talk. Some, seated at tables, had paper in front of them, some had maps of the county spread out, others had their laptops open and keyboards busy. Business was now being seriously conducted, either in preliminary or finalizing stages.

The flurry of men gathered around 'Coops' and 'Georgie Boy's' table were growing to three deep. And the decibels of talk were greatest from that area as by now most men had realized that these two members of the Franklinite Group held the key to deals, to business activity, to profits, and to on-going well-being for those who were both clever enough and sharp enough to finalize land options or even close deals, construction deals, and property management deals for buildings yet to be designed, approved, financed, built and sold over the ensuing months and years as the National Park Service moved toward fulfilling its move from Washington to the Great Central Valley of California.

I caught a glimpse of Randy Rhodes as he, too, at his table, had become even more an equally important focus of attention.

I could imagine him thinking that from here on out the political leader Jewell Nightingale might pay him more attention, put him in touch with more important people in Washington, and at the least smile warmly at him, maybe even including him in important lunches and arrange for him exciting and meaningful introductions with important influential government people.

In the midst of my observations and musings, I heard Heck's counsel. My secret friend was saying to me, *"Do you realize, Buddy Boy, that none of this information about the move of this federal agency to the Central Valley has been confirmed, verified, substantiated, and how else can I say it? Has there been anything in the 'Congressional Record?'"*

I told Heck I didn't subscribe, but allowed as how maybe now was the time to go to our county library and search through that publication's recent issues, or maybe it's online. But, for sure, I posed Heck's doubts to my friend Dave and to Judge Jim, as well as Pete Peterson.

Their responses were along the line that, as Dave summed up, "Listen, we here today and tonight have been let in on a very important development in the federal government by someone who is the position to know about this development. In advance, I might add. And out of loyalty to his Congressional District and his loyalty to us in this extended community of ranchers, businessmen, educators, civic, and religious leaders. I mean, no one is going to make something like this up out of thin air. Don't you all agree with me on this point?"

I thought my friend was, as surveyors needed to be, level headed. I mean, surveyors can leave no room for imagination as they plot exact lines and boundaries. As with few other professions, the exact truth is their rallying point of beginning and concluding. I reminded myself that gone were the days of laying out a parcel of land with something called chains and using old trees as markers, guessing at distances, more or less. Today, surveying is a science. It is a compendium of mathematical truths. "Argue with that," I implored Heck.

He came back with, *"So then, we are just going to lay over and accept what Randy Rhodes tells us as 'Gospel'?"*

Again, I looked around the hall and thought about the matter for a moment before I said, "Yes" as I polished off my bottle of beer. Then I corrected myself and said out loud to Heck and to myself a resounding "no!"

CHAPTER 28

Congresswoman and Party Leader
Jewell Nightingale

———

Obviously not satisfied with my knowledge of politics, I decided that it was imperative that I know more about Jewell Nightingale. What influence was she in this game? Without question, she was becoming an important key player in the drama being orchestrated here today by Randy Rhodes. But, apart from her political position, who really is she?

To find out more about this leader of a national political party, I fetched my lap top from my vehicle intending to access her official website. First, however, I googled her name to see what websites and information might come up. Facebook, Linked In and other social media sites were full of her photographs. Since hers was an unusual name combination, there was no one competing for Internet attention with either the same or even a similar name.

The array of photographs took the viewer—that's me—back to the time she was a student in high school. A bevy of female and male friends, and her pet, a large beautifully colored and quite cuddly fury Bernese Mountain Dog, along with a few smiling older folks who could have been parents or teachers. Each came and went as I flipped across the social media sites. The breed of dog seemed appropriate to me, for I quickly learned from her curriculum vitae that Jewell was a native of the Appalachian Mountains of western North Carolina that formed the pinnacled and crenellated backbone of the Eastern U.S. running from Georgia north to Maine and Mount Katahdin. Jewell hailed from a county right on the border with Tennessee. This particular county had been part of the collection of counties that had made up the here-today-gone-tomorrow state of Franklin in the late 1700s.

I then clicked on Jewell's personal website and learned from her stated background that she had graduated from a rural high school where she had been active in political party politics, even at that relatively early time in her life. After high school, she had enrolled in the regional community college, taking courses, so her website boasted, in civics and political science.

I switched to her official Congressional website. There it told how, while still in school, she had joined the staff of the state-operated rustic lodge popular with backpackers high atop Mount Le Conte, the highest summit in North Carolina. There, she had worked a number of assignments, including leading the supply chain of Llamas up the mountain carrying in their panniers the necessary food and other supplies to keep the lodge running, for there were no roads leading to the lodge. An avid mountain person, she was quoted as advising compatriots at the lodge, as well as, even today, her fellow legislators with the by-now famous quote, "When in doubt, run up hill."

Another URL caught my eye. It was dubbed "Little known tidbits about your Congressman or woman." Googling in her name, and then regretting my action, feeling as if I were prying upon her privacy, the site told how one night among the guests who had hiked up Mount Le Conte with their full backpacks and were staying in the lodge, Jewell met this man who was important in her political party's hierarchy. They soon struck up a conversation about Jewell's future life in the party, to which she expressed her complete loyalty, both ideologically, as well as to its leadership.

The next morning, and here the author seemed to get carried away with his or her knowledge of fog, for he or she explained that in the Appalachians the fog comes in like a marching band at half time, whereas the fog in California's Central Valley either creeps in from the Pacific on little cat's feet or mystically rises from the tule grass. At any rate, Jewell and the man hiked that morning. Soon he was asking her to come join his staff at the governor's office in Raleigh, which she did.

Later on, he had run and been elected to Congress, and she had become his staff assistant. They had planned to be married when tragedy struck. He perished in an airplane accident. Soon the governor appointed her to serve out his unexpired term. From there, exercising her political connections as well as drawing on her support in her home county, she had been elected by a narrow margin to the Congressional seat. Repeated victories every two years led to her serving a series of terms, allowing for her to rise in party hierarchy and become a party leader in Congress.

That Jewell had never married became apparent when reading more. As to her family, there was mention of her parents who were still living in the mountains of North Carolina. She had one sibling, a sister who was married and living in Silicon Valley. Her personal credo, as quoted on her website, advised high school students to become interested in government, to register to vote, and to become active in party politics."

* * *

By now, the guys at the round table had all left to circulate among the participants. I had no one with whom to share my findings. That is, other than Heck, who suggested, *"Let's find out from Randy Rhodes when Jewell Nightingale is next coming to the Central Valley."*

CHAPTER 29

Pressing On

———

I acknowledged Heck's assignment. I then sought out both the editor of the daily newspaper, Jim Early, and Randy Rhodes. Seeing Early first, I made my way to his side and posed the question as to what he made out of Rhodes' valley-shaking announcement.

"He smiled as if he knew something not fit to print and told me, "We've been trying to get a second confirmation, you know. That is, a verification from a second credible source with knowledge of the matter. But in calling both Congressman Shultz' office and Ms. Nightingale's office, we got only the messages that they were with other Congressmen and women on a factfinding mission somewhere in the Middle East and wouldn't return for several days. However, in my talking directly to Rhodes," and he pointed toward a large gathering of men some distance away, "I was admonished by him that, and I quote, 'It's premature to make any media announcement at this time.'"

"But," I said, "he's announced his news all over the place here in this hall today. I mean, how many people have heard him tell us about the federal agency relocating here?"

"I know, but proper journalism rules are rules, my friend. You wouldn't have it otherwise, would you?"

"So, you're just going to listen to rumors, if that's what you call Randy's formal announcement. After all, he is—"

"—Yeah, yeah." The newspaper and TV man leaned close and whispered, his tone conveying a confidence, "You know, Randy's done this sort of thing before."

"The same announcement?" I queried.

"No, no, but on a story of similarly presumed importance… two years ago…he told a group of reporters at a breakfast meeting here that the FBI was going to open an academy for special training of recruits with a separate section for advanced senior agents to train in more clandestine operations. But, again, we couldn't confirm it. And the story went by the boards. Nothing ever came of it, try as we might to verify his tip on this bit of significance news."

"But, Mr. Early, every one of these men here today and this evening and tonight are going to leave this hall—whenever they do so tonight or tomorrow—and they're going to tell everyone in their families, their businesses, their friends they see in the next few days about this news—or is it rumor? I mean, it is going to be the talk in every bar, and in Sunday on every church or synagogue, mosque, or Buddhist meditation group, and among the wait staff and the patrons at the CVA club…I don't want to even mention the bowling alleys."

Early nodded, smiled at me in a sort of confirmation, suggesting, "You forgot to list the Legion Hall," and he moved off toward the big corrugated cooler loaded with more beer.

Heck told me, *"You had better contact Congressman Shultz or, better still, party leader Jewell Nightingale and tell her what is going on here."*

I told my secret friend, "Early just said they tried with several phone calls and each time were told they're both off to the Middle East on some Congressional jaunt. If I call, I'll get the same answer."

Heck suggested, *"Try a different source—like, maybe, the federal agency itself—the National Park Service. They'll have a public relations person somewhere in their bureaucracy."*

Reaching for my phone but then realizing, I exclaimed, "Uh oh, there's a three-hour time difference between here and D.C. I'll get an answering machine."

"Then leave a callback number." Indeed, Heck was expressing his usual persistence. So, I called, asked to speak to the Congresswoman, and was promptly told that Ms. Nightingale was on a bi-partisan fact-finding mission in the Middle East. Thanking the operator, I left my name and call back number, as Heck had instructed.

Just then, Dave went by, so I stopped him to relate the new developments I had learned from media man Jim Early about Randy Rhodes.

Dave didn't act surprised, for he came back with, "Yeah, many guys here rate Randy's reliance as borderline when it comes to this sort of information."

I was a bit stunned, as I'm sure was Heck. I said, "But no one challenged him when he was talking. I mean no one stood up and called out 'bullshit' or something else."

"No one would dare do that to him."

"Why not?"

Randy is our live link. He is always readily available for information into some aspect of the government and its agencies 3000 miles away in Washington. And, of course, he's in daily contact with our Congressman. No one wants to turn off that spicket of information and certainly not his ready and waiting introductions to business contacts important to those of us here in the Central Valley. If we need something, we'll call Randy and, presto, we've got it. At least, most of the time. No one wants to cut off such a reliable source of information. Accordingly, we will, I guess you might say, humor him a bit. Not one of us dares cross him and garner criticism from others in our community for having done so, let alone make an enemy of Randy."

Heck said to me, "*Truth takes a backseat when it comes to the federal government, I conclude from all this.*"

Of course, Dave didn't hear Heck's remark to me, but he added his comment to our conversation, "You know, my friend, it seems that more and more today truth has become an obsolete word."

I troubled over the whole situation as I stood there looking after my surveyor friend Dave as he went for another beer. I called after him, "But we can't just let this rumor or announcement fester." As he returned, I added, "And slowly float away like the Central Valley morning fog when the sun comes out."

To my surprise, Dave pointed toward the front glass double entry doors of the hall and said, "I just saw Randy Rhodes leave the building, car keys in hand, so he's gone, maybe for good, maybe until later."

Surprised at his exit, I wondered to myself how many deals had been made between men here that were reacting and counting monetarily on Randy's announcement? I asked Dave, "How many bets have bene placed, how much money, if any, has changed hands based on Randy's wild rumor?"

He replied, "Oh, I wouldn't worry about that. This here's the Central Valley, not Silicon Valley where deals are made, so I understand, on the backs of envelopes and even more quickly on tablet computers, by word of mouth, a wink of the eye, and all the while based on someone's anticipated hope, gut feeling, or the dazzle in their eyes.

"Folks here don't rush out and do things on the spur of the moment. If you've lived here as long as I have, you'll get used to thinking ideas and deals through backwards and forwards and then, maybe once again, and then maybe you just sleep on the matter and let it turn over in your mind several times. I mean, decisions here are like our crops. They take time to grow. That's why our harvests are so valuable, precious, and the envy of farmers everywhere."

"Rip Van Winkle's nap lasted forty years."

Dave laughed. "Sometimes it seems that long for some people here to decide on something, but not really. Folks here have alarm clocks and cell phones that, sooner or later, buzz them into action."

Heck told me to do something, but he didn't say what. So, I implored Dave, "I feel I must do something to either verify this rumor or put it to sleep for 40 years."

Dave was going to turn away and move on through the hall, I could tell from his fidgeting, but then, hearing my words, he stopped and stood stationary as he thought for a moment. Soon he said, "Tell you what, my friend, let's do this. I've an idea—just came to me."

"And?"

"Well, this is an idea that's going to have to think itself."

"Go on," I pleaded.

"Okay, here goes: Jewell Nightingale's older sister, Emma, I believe is her name, is married to this high-tech engineer who is one of the group of founders of an AI startup in Silicon Valley. You know, this new field of artificial intelligence?"

"That's where they, or their mysterious super computers generate the ideas that think themselves, that is, without your and my help," I suggested.

Dave chuckled. "I read a news article about the company. It was not written by a human, for I couldn't understand a thing, other than there seemed to be another level of thinking out there that was beyond me. I guess that's artificial intelligence."

"Where does our own personal intelligence fit into all this?" I asked.

Heck suggested, *"Takes human intelligence to make artificial intelligence."*

Dave said, "Let's get back to Jewell Nightingale, "Jewell's sister and her high-tech husband have twin daughters who are already in kindergarten."

"I'm getting the picture."

"Jewell's father is retired from his job at a furniture manufacturer in North Carolina. He and her mother miss their grandkids a great deal. I mean, who wouldn't these days?"

"Miss grandkids," I agreed, adding, "especially when they're 3,000 miles away."

"You got it. But wait, there's more to this story, right here today. You see, our retired Marine Lt. Col. Hammill, who I think you met earlier, lives in an active adult retirement community not far from here. He told me that Jewell's parents had visited his community wanting to scope out a place to retire so that they could be closer to the twins."

I asked, "The Colonel has met Jewell?"

"Yes, he showed her and her parents around his community and introduced them to a number of his friends, as well as showing them the many craft facilities, plus the pool and exercise equipment and, oh yes, the library. They were appreciative of his hospitality and agreed to stay in touch."

"Nice," I suggested, wondering where Dave's idea was leading him.

Dave went on, "The Colonel told me a few minutes ago that Jewell is coming with them to visit and perhaps help them buy a place. He said that while his community may not be in Silicon Valley itself, it is close enough so that her parents can visit their grandchildren more frequently, certainly than if they remained back east in North Carolina. To boot, in my opinion, there's Jewell's connection to the Franklinites here at our CVA club. She could introduce her parents into that circle."

I said, "But Jewell is off in the Middle East right now, as her office told you and, just a few minutes ago, also told me."

Dave said, "Yes, but that's not where she really is. She's actually in Washington, and is on her way here with her parents, arriving tonight, so I understand from what Colonel Hammill told me. She doesn't want anyone to know she's escorting her parents on a trip, so her office put up the smoke screen as to her whereabouts. I have heard that a lot of people in government broadcast that sort of clandestine deception so that their actual location remains a secret from trouble makers, lobbyists, and the press. That's so that they can seek personal privacy."

I pressed Dave, "So, where does this idea of yours think it will lead us?"

"Why not to a meeting of you and I with Jewell, as arranged by our friend Col. Hamill, either tonight or tomorrow?"

"Okay," I replied enthusiastically. "Let's pigeonhole the colonel and set up a get-together for tonight or tomorrow."

* * *

Moments later, having wended my way through the crowded hall, I came up to Lt. Col. Hammill. Again, I was impressed by his erect posture which spoke to his career discipline of sporting a military bearing. Once a Marine, always a Marine, I reminded myself. I was so taken with his sense of presence that I found myself wanting to salute him. Then I thought the Army's salute is a bit different from the Marine's and I didn't want to invoke his reprimand for not properly executing the military maneuver of mutual respect between an officer and an enlisted man, so I simply smiled and addressed him as

Colonel. I'd leave the salute up to Heck.

I said, "Colonel, my surveyor friend Dave just told me you will be meeting Jewell Nightingale and her parents this evening."

He replied promptly, "Why yes, that is so. I want to discuss with them and Jewell her parent's possible move into my retirement community. It's nearby, you know. Her parents are a delightful couple—he's retired Army, and I will always go out of my way to help a fellow veteran." He added, "As to Jewell, she is a powerful and effective woman, being high up in party politics nationally."

"That's very good of you…I mean, as to her parents, Sir."

"But, young man, I don't run the retirement community. Rather, I am simply a resident, having been there a number of years since my wife passed away. That's when I sold our home and held one of those downsizing estate sales. Right away, I bought a nice little apartment in my new community. Did I tell you that My Lady and I were married more than 50 wonderful years in my long military career. We're apart now, of course, but I'm planning to rejoin her when I pass away, you know?"

I found myself nodding. Perplexed, however, I pondered for a moment what it would be like losing a partner, especially after so many years. I wanted to ask him, but then I guess maybe I knew his answer from the description he had offered telling me of his intention to eventually rejoin her.

"We'll be together again," the colonel went on to reiterate, as if he were plotting his Marine battalion's prospective military field maneuver.

Trying to return to the subject of meeting Jewell, I prompted myself to ask, "Sir, would it be possible for Dave and me to meet Jewell Nightingale, as I want to ask her about Randy Rhodes' announcement today? I mean, in talking with the men here, I've learned that some discount Randy's announcement as being simply a rumor.

They cite his past record of sometimes displaying a lack of credibility, and mention a number of unconfirmed, what they are calling 'his wild stories.'"

"Meet them? Oh yes, for sure you two can do that."

I handed the Colonel my business card and Dave's, as well, and asked precisely when and where, as if Dave and I were to be players in carrying out his military maneuver.

He replied, "Well, before Randy Rhodes left the hall, he told me he was on his way to meet the airport shuttle at, and let me look at my watch…yes… it'll be in about an hour or so, I should think. Right downtown, that is, at the front gate of the CVA Club—that's the shuttle's regular stop. I've taken it several times back and forth to the international airport, almost always on time, it is."

"Will they be coming here?"

"Oh no. Randy has booked a suite of guest rooms for them at my retirement community." The Colonel smiled proudly and explained further, "We have a small luxury inn for visiting prospective owners."

Heck instructed, *"Plot your next move, Buddy Boy?"*

Meanwhile, the Colonel was explaining further, "Our…it's called 'The Haven.' It is run by retired volunteers who live in our community. They're hospitality folks who find it hard in retirement to give up the day-to-day challenges of real life." Then he added, "It's like I wanted to practice our Marine daily routine on our picnic grounds to solemnly blow 'taps' on a loud speaker every evening at 5 o'clock and then salute the stars and stripes. Alas, my plan to do so was turned down by our peace-loving Board of Directors." Always a Marine, he shook his head in disbelief at their expressed lack of patriotism. He stressed to me, "You know, the ceremony is in respect for those gallant men and women who gave their life for their country."

I smiled, suggesting sympathy with the distinguished veteran's point of view and then pressed, "Ah, Colonel, how then can Dave and I meet Jewell and her parents?"

"Oh, I'm going to meet the shuttle and drive them. It's just a few miles, you know."

"Will, you be coming by here on your way?"

"I shouldn't think so. Why do you ask?"

Softly I replied, "We want to meet them."

"Oh, that's right. He thought for a moment and then said, "Well, so yes, so I'll call you when we leave the shuttle stop and you two can be standing tall at the front door of our hall here."

I felt like saying, Jolly good," but then thought better of it. Instead, I advised the Colonel I would await his call. In agreement with that idea, he nodded and soon left the hall.

Heck warned with his question, *"Can we count on the retired Colonel, or will he forget?"*

* * *

As time went by inside the hall, Dave and I waited rather impatiently and with anticipation for my cell to buzz with a message from the Marine officer at the airport shuttle drop off point. My phone had a vibrator in case I missed the ring, like in a restaurant when you are waiting for that little box they hand out that will soon announce your table is ready. I was glad I had done that because here in the crowded convention hall, given that the conversations among the men were quite loud, I was afraid I might miss the sound of the Colonel's incoming call. In the meantime, I imagined that the men here were conversing about their ideas for taking advantage of Randy Rhodes' valley-shaking announcement about the National Park Service relocating its national headquarters from Washington, D. C. to this part of the Central Valley.

Some were probably trying to negotiate land purchase options for anticipated housing and commercial developments, while others were putting in their oars for contracts relating to a burgeoning demand for new developments of all sorts. I saw Father Isadore talking to—I presumed a parishioner of his church— likely about the need for a site for a new sanctuary to serve a growing influx from back east of his faithful. Surely such an in-migration of the devout was to come to pass. The architect I had met earlier was now joining them.

Then, as if in a restaurant awaiting notice my order was ready, I received the announcing buzz from my cell, followed quickly by its ring. It was indeed the Colonel advising that their "convoy" was departing ground zero and would soon arrive outside the hall. "The convoy is on its way," I repeated to Dave, who acted as surprised with the use of the term as I was.

Dave thought for a moment and then suggested, "The Colonel and Randy Rhodes—maybe they have two cars."

CHAPTER 30

The Black SUV Convoy

———

"Convoy," I repeated the word, showing my surprise. In response to the Colonel's phone message, Dave and I moved through the men toward the glass double entry doors. In only a few moments, we could see four pitch-black large SUVs approaching the entry to the hall. They came to a full stop outside the hall entry, lining up side by side, as if in military formation.

"Four SUVs", Dave remarked in disbelief, the feeling Heck echoed.

I could see emblazoned on the doors of each vehicle the insignia of a federal agency with the words "U. S. police" appended. As well, I could see that each SUV bore U.S. government license plates. From the first vehicle, and actually from all four, dark-suited uniformed agents simultaneously jumped out and stood at attention, gloved hands clutching door handles, prepared upon signal to open each vehicle's passenger door.

I wondered out loud to Dave, "Who and how many passengers are riding in these vehicles?" With eyebrows raised, he shared my curiosity.

Passengers from the first vehicle were first to exit. They were led by a tall man in a well-pressed National Park Service ranger uniform. He was wearing the traditional park ranger hat, broad brimmed, with the crown having a soft crease down the middle. Looking at Dave and me and smiling at each of us, he held out his hand expecting us to follow suit, which we did. As we shook, he announced in a pleasant historic-marker-sounding voice, "I'm Ranger Rick Newcastle, head of the National Park Service. With me today are Congresswoman Jewell Nightingale and her parents."

They exited their SUV, saw us, and nodded our way. Ranger Rick, added, "And from the other vehicles are members of my staff." By now the staff members were decanting themselves from the remaining vehicles, their doors being held open by the uniformed drivers. Each staff member clutched a black leather briefcase as if they were prepared, upon call, to deliver some sort of governmental presentation.

My gaze was immediately drawn to Jewell Nightingale who, flashing an alluring smile, stepped around Ranger Rick to extend her hand toward Dave and then me. With smiles of welcome, we shook.

The Congressional leader was attractively attired in keeping with being a prominent member of her political party. She promptly introduced her parents from North Carolina and told us how much her family appreciated this opportunity to hopefully arrange for the purchase of a home in Colonel Hamill's nearby lovely retirement community, "Where we are headed, following our brief 'touch base' with 'y'all' and the men in this convention hall," to which she pointed and moved to enter, her entourage in tow, including, right behind her, the attending Randy Rhodes.

Dave whispered to me, "So, after all, Randy Rhodes was giving us the straight poop."

I nodded my agreement. Wasting no time in speaking to Ranger Newcastle, I said, "So, you and your agency are going to relocate here, lock, stock, and barrel?"

The head of all park rangers everywhere held up his hand and said, "Let me hasten to clarify our mission for you."

"Please," Dave and I said, almost in unison and in anticipatory tones of voice.

The federal government head man from the Nation's Capital took the two of us aside, as the others in his entourage filed through the double glass entry doors. Ranger Rick said, "Our mission, which we are now pursuing with our visit here, is to investigate several possible sites across the country. The Great Central Valley is our first stop. But it is only one choice, as there are several others 'out west,' as they say.

I heard another *"uh oh"* from Heck.

I asked, "Where are the other areas of your interest?"

The head ranger appeared intent on entering the hall. He looked annoyed at me and quipped, "Oh, I'm not authorized to divulge that information."

As he passed through the glass double entry doors, I said to Dave, "Let's sick Jim Early on him to see if, given Jim's journalistic skills, he can extract more bits of information."

Dave agreed and we set off, once inside the hall, to find the KROP man.

Meanwhile, the visiting delegation was entering the hall.

* * *

Looking around inside, I spotted Jewell Nightingale and her parents. Again, I was consumed by her appearance, her stylish attire, along with the warm message I sensed she was exuding to those around her. Indeed, she was engaged in several conversations, alternating from one to the other, while several other men waited impatiently to speak to her. I was left with saying some nice welcoming message to her parents while Dave wandered off to find our media journalist.

After we introduced ourselves, Jewell's father said to me, "I haven't seen so many men in one place since my friends in the Sons of the Confederacy recreated one of their forced marches through Appalachia several years ago.

I ventured to ask, "You a member?"

He nodded, "My great grandfather fought in one of the last battles of the Second War for Independence. That was in Columbia, South Carolina right dab at the end."

I hummed the tune, "'The Day They Put Old Dixie Down,'" and then, contradicting, suggested, "The Civil War."

"He smiled. "Whatever label you prefer."

Mrs. Nightingale said her name was Tarra, and I should call her that, which I did, by saying, "I understand you're looking for a retirement home in Colonel Hammill's community."

She smiled and confirmed, adding, "His community, just like mine at home, has a lovely garden club. The Colonel graciously introduced us to the horticulturists running the club."

He clarified, "That was on our first visit."

I explored, "Say, do you know where Ranger Newcastle is headed when he and his staff leave here?"

Mr. Nightingale answered, "He said not to tell anyone."

Heck said, *"They know. Press the question."*

"Is it in California?"

Tarra asked, "Where's—"

Her husband silenced her with the palm of his hand raised toward her.

She said, "But I'm not disclosing any secrets. just tell me where is Jefferson?"

"Jefferson?" I repeated, showing confusion.

Tarra nodded.

Mr. Nightingale tried to clarify, "She means the state of, but there isn't any state with that name."

Heck said, *"Tell her it's at the end of the yellow brick road."*

"No," I told Heck, "She is Jewell's mother. I want to be polite to her."

Heck insisted, *"But the state of that name doesn't exist."*

The light dawning suddenly, I said to Tarra, "Yes, the state of Jefferson. It's in southern Oregon and Northern California, but only in the fantasies of some folks. It's like the state of Franklin, a name, but only from yesteryear."

Tarra said, "But that's where the head ranger and his troupe are going next."

"And Jewel is going with them?"

"Oh, yes, of course she is."

I thought that meant Southern Oregon, Ashland and Medford. And there's a major airport in Medford. Plus, a lot of land and a college. Agriculture, too…not unlike the attributes of the Central Valley.

Heck asked, *"And what other areas are like that, as well? Think about that for a minute."*

Taking Heck's advice, which I often did, I felt a pattern for Ranger Newcastle's visit was emerging.

* * *

At that moment, Dave joined our group. Jim Early was with him. Jewell was, too.

Seeing Jewell again, I thought how some people seem to exhibit a sense of presence beyond the usual and above the norm. When your eyes and their eyes meet, just between the two of you, a certain electricity seems to connect in a flash verifying a certain camaraderie, a note playing on the same octave, a buzz like in my cell phone when a call is coming in—a vibration. I somehow felt that way with Jewell. Of course, I had no idea how she felt, for to date we had only exchanged a handshake and cursory smiles.

Perhaps all this is a trait of really successful folks—they are able, or maybe it comes naturally to them—to communicate in this extra-sensory perception. For with Jewell, when she came into a room and joined the presence of other people, she immediately stood out. She was not a tag along but instead a leader. If there had been a battlefield, you would automatically follow her command to charge, weapon ready, helmet affixed and determination becoming your motivational inspiration.

Maye it was because I had read her website and had familiarized myself with her background, read her story and felt a oneness with her accomplishments, she coming from a rural Appalachian backwater area, or maybe that was unfair to characterize her home ground that way. I wanted to apologize to her. Or maybe I was just simply attracted to her. Nothing wrong with that, I suppose, except I didn't know what Heck might make of it. Can you, I asked myself, have secrets from your secret friend?

Enough, for here she was, looking at me, and yes, also at Dave and Jim Early, who had, I presumed, already introduced himself to her and to her parents.

It was at that moment, like a lightning bolt, that I recalled a brief article I had once read. It was written by a clergyman, who had been asked to characterize certain exceptional people he had met. He said something along the same lines as my mind had just expressed, adding that his take on the question had to do with the traits he felt his Savior possessed—clearly above the run of the mill pundit and leader of his time. For, this minister had written, asking the devout to look at what happened with this man, to consider what he had accomplished and what events following had endured his name to us world-wide and across the centuries of time.

Suddenly I found myself speechless in our little group inside the much larger group of men in this convention hall. Somehow, I heard Jewell's voice speaking to us. She was saying, "Would you gentlemen have it any other way?"

What had she just said? I asked Heck, but heard nothing back. I asked Dave, and he looked at me as if I was out of it. But then, taking pity, I supposed, overcoming my mental absence, he took me aside and filled me in on her words, causing me to reflect back in time, my personal time.

CHAPTER 31

My Memoir

———

Someday soon, I promised myself, I would begin to write my memoirs. They would be a re-telling of my emotions during my many-year career of real estate development: my experiences in optioning or buying land parcels, getting development approvals from the authorities, in finding financing, lining up sub-contractors, and then building the homes. But my memoirs wouldn't stop there, for I had to sell the homes to buyers, and that required knowing the true person with whom I was negotiating, their real interests, their desires, over and beyond their outward appearing demands and the words they would toss my way—in other words getting to know their true selfs.

The memoir would be full of true experiences in the world of real estate development, finance, design, and building techniques. Hopefully by the time I got to writing my memoir, I would also have achieved financial success.

Heck would edit, of course, and throw in his comments and observations, his judgments of my decisions.

Among the real estate episodes, I would tell the one that I had now experienced, which I had received vibes from Jewell Nightingale and her attentive helper, Randy Rhodes. But this particular story would go back a few years in time to when self-propelled motor homes and manufactured mobile homes had become the latest fad of manufacturing in the Midwest. It was in Indiana, geographically centered. In a race to increase their market share, these specialized manufacturers were looking for new sites in towns where the labor supply was readily available, probably non-union and not expensive in their hourly wages, as their profit margins were geared to maximizing assembly line efficiencies and cost controls.

The men running the town were always vying for importance, by building their personal recognition, that is, becoming the big man on campus, so to speak. One of these men, not unlike the men in this convention hall here today, heard about this particular manufacturer that was searching for a site to build a large facility.

Being a real estate investor, he either owned or had options on a large tract of land on the edge of town next to a railroad siding and with easy freeway access for parts and for shipping finished products. He approached the manufacturer, offering his site to them at what he deemed to be an attractive and profitable price for himself.

The company grew interested but told him they were considering other towns. Panicking, he lowered his price and, in addition, offered to build them the plant, leasing it to them on favorable terms. Being influential in his community, he persuaded the county tax collector to waive property taxes for a number of years, and the sales tax authorities in the state government in Indianapolis not to charge sales taxes on the completed units for five years.

They balked. He sweetened his offer. They negotiated. He made them a better offer. By now, had he taken time to figure it out, his loss from this deal had grown quite high. after they accepted his offer, and he became the town hero for having attracted this new industry to town with its ever so many jobs, he recalculated his costs.

All through his bankruptcy, he remained a town hero, his success at bringing the new facility to town enabled him to have a statue erected to him in the town square.

And this is the story Dave was beginning to tell me, except I knew it already. It was a re-play of the episode of the over-eager developer. And I realized what Jewell Nightingale was up to. I suspected that Randy Rhodes may have been in on some aspect of the scheme. For sure, though other Congressional Aids in other Congressional districts in other areas of the country were finding out about this rumor and dutifully telling certain developers in their districts about it. The NACA—"

Heck intoned, *"The National Association of Congressional Aides."*

I nodded, continuing, "NACA would probably disclaim any knowledge of the plan. Nevertheless, real estate developers would promptly be competing for land options or purchases and for contracts to build houses and commercial facilities in the hope of winning a deal and, in their new and enhanced reputation, becoming their area's big man on campus.

* * *

Nevertheless, I couldn't help admire Jewell's scheme. The idea was in keeping with her moto expressed to those in the Le Conte Inn high atop Mont Le Conte in her native North Carolina: when in doubt, run up hill. For her, this scheme was indeed an uphill one.

BOOK TWO

CHAPTER 32

Years Later
Where is My Secret Friend?

———

Heck has left my side; in fact, it has been some time, as I reflect back on the passing years. I must confess, I have realized how lonely I have been without him. On days like today, when I get that deep-down sinking feeling in my emotions, there is no one by my side to bolster my outlook, no one to set me straight in my thinking as Heck was wont so often to do from the time when we met. I was about 12 years old. And he had stayed with me, I with him, through…yes…it was up into my forties.

The last time Heck contributed so importantly to my life was in the Central Valley of California, a time when I was building houses, or wanting to build houses, seeking that way of life to make a living.

But now that I am older, I find myself most often by myself. I garner no advice from Heck, who was for all those days, weeks, months and, yes, even years, my secret friend. But now I receive no daily directions. Furthermore, so I do admit, I no longer benefit from Heck's frank and, I always deemed, constructive criticisms of me, my ideas, and my actions. As a result of this void, I receive no encouragement, no instructions, so that I have been on my own for

162 | The Idea Which Thinks Itself

the past bundle of years. And so today, I ask, indeed I plead: Where is my secret friend Heck?

During the days, weeks, and months of our not being together, has he aged along with me? That surely can't be, for Heck, I am certain, at least so I feel, has remained young, even as I have grown older. During this transition of our being apart, he has not advised me on my attitudes toward life and my feelings toward my fellow beings, or so it seems to me, creating a void in my life, a blank spot in my emotions. That is so true, especially on the dark days when I must live with my loneliness. In his outlook and in his advice, Heck was always young and as enthusiastic as a high school cheer leader at the Big Game—you know, on the day we tore the goalposts down.

I do so miss Heck. I was thinking about him just this morning on my uphill walk. He used to urge me on, but this morning I was having difficulty urging myself upward. Twice I considered bagging my daily morning ritual and just sitting on that bench by my favorite tree, waiting for my favorite bird to land on its top branch. But today the bird and Heck were nowhere to be either seen or heard.

During my sitting on the convenient bench, pausing in my climb, I did ponder the thought as to whether Heck has aged along with me? Well, for sure, doesn't everybody age, flowers, animals, my favorite little bird, the trees, and the universe, too, I suppose? If that is true, which I believe it to be, then why is Heck, having aged along with me, not by my side, especially during this morning's walk? If he hasn't aged, or even if he has, then why has he not kept pace with me in my advancing age? Or if he, being somewhere else, has changed so as to no longer care about me?

I have confided to other men, and some women, about my secret friend Heck, only to learn, when our conversations went deep down sufficiently for secrets to be aired, that that they, too, once had a secret friend, or maybe still do. At some time in their lives, that friend had helped them navigate experiences and changes in their lives, such as childhood experiences, entering and navigating grade school, then high school, agreeing to their marriage, perhaps, and as well applying for and then pursuing their job, and later helping out in pursuing their career.

But then I had to ask them and myself, as well, if secret friends are a time-only thing? Is it that they are with you for a while, the length depending on the person, before they then vanish into the sunset? Do they possibly return or have they already moved on? If so, maybe they have become someone else's secret friend, befriending a new companion, at that time or even at a later date? Once, and maybe twice, or how often, if at all, do they do that? Is that the lifestyle of a secret friend—and has it been that way for my secret friend Heck? And for all secret friends, going back to the beginning? The beginning of what? To the beginning of the uncertainties of life, of society, of personal survival, of personal well-being…the need for advice, the need for companionship, the need for personal perspective as to one's own self? Yes, it must be that way, or so I concluded. But who will verify my conclusion, and how will someone confirm my understanding?

I had sort of, albeit reluctantly, come to accept the fact that, as my life advanced, things do not stay the same. That concept is expressed in the one word that some label as "impermanence." Life, everyone's life, as well as the world around us, moves on. So, I ask: has Heck joined this movement of moving on, and in the process moved away from me? Back then, we were so close, almost loving each other, so it seems in hindsight, but more importantly I was personally benefiting from his companionship, his advice, his thoughts on ever so many topics at hand. I was moving upward in life as I assimilated his wisdom. Now, I lack additions to that wisdom, brought on by a change in my circumstances as I approach the retirement years. Therein lies my fear of this morning as I sit on the park bench, urging myself on to resume my uphill walk.

Looking at the theory of history, as I get up from the bench and resume my upward steps, I realize that history is also herstory. History has painted shades of colors, genders, and backgrounds. Yet it has not always been that way, but it is so now, and that is one story of how impermanence changes everything, including the flow of our lives.

Has this concept of impermanence taken Heck from me? I mean, have our heroes of yesteryear changed—some leaving, while we add new ones—some with different skin colors and others with different genders, some with orientation to life new to me in their descriptions and in their interests.

Have these ideas and the changes that have adjusted my life taken Heck from me?

Is he there only in the past, far before the present? Am I in the present or am I nostalgic for the past, or—if I have given up the past, am I entering a new life in a new and freshly revised present moment?

I mean, if Heck was with me in the past but not here now, then was the past moment or moments a figure of my imagination, or is the present moment being imagined? And if so, then Heck, out of sorts with me, cannot be here now with me. Or am I mistaken on that point?

But I think he isn't here now, as he says nothing, and advises me on nothing. He is silent, that is, if he is here, and that is not how Heck was in the past. Therefore, he is not here now, or so I conclude. Unless, I imagine him here, but even if I imagine him here now, and he is not here, then he is not here, is he?

Oh, where is he? If he is existing somewhere at all? Was my imagination running wild in those past moments? Or was my imagination then a reality in some sort of special frame of mind, both mine and his, back then in those valuable distant days?

I could call out, loudly and persistently, right now this moment, but will I hear a response to my summons, or is it better characterized as a pleading? Yes, I'll try to do so. And I just did. But in response there is only silence. Nada. Nothing. And now all I hear is the same on-going void of silence.

I know. I shall sit quietly, once again, perhaps meditate, perhaps imagine, perhaps wish, perhaps yearn, all emotions summoning Heck to be by my side, to be with me here now.

I did each of those things for the remainder of the day. And the result? The same. No Heck. No voice. No counsel. No companionship. Only the loneliness of silence, of being by myself. The isolation of isolation. The nothing of nothing. I gave up, but thought I might try on the morrow. Perhaps my earnestness is lacking. Maybe my sincerity is weak. Maybe Heck is not coming back. Maybe Heck is nowhere now. Maybe I'll never see or talk to Heck again…treasure the past…for it is deposited in my archive of memories. Memories of excitement. Memories of happiness. Memories to be treasured and called upon at appropriate times, when ready, when steeled for the disappointment and maybe even the failure of recalling memories—being fixed, carved in stone, not to be revived, and not to be lived again at any time in the present time.

CHAPTER 33

Where is Heck?
Here I am, But First I Must Tell You

———

Folks may want to know about the legend of secret friends. Being one of these Delphic personages, my name is Heck. I am a secret friend. Many secret friends, in addition to me, float about. We assign ourselves to a person, or maybe the person assigns one of us to them. Either way, we do our duty, in our own unique way, to advise our person, to put their lives, their opinions, their desires into a perspective that they feel and appreciate. Our goal is to improve them beyond their true selves.

It is said by some, although not by me, that we realized our genesis in one or more of Shakespeare's plays, wherein he wrote that in every royal court there was a wise joker. The joker's role was to put the king's selfish idiosyncrasies into perspective through the joker's humor and invitation to comment. In other words, to act as a licensed, or authorized, contrarian to the king's whims. The king and those at court allowed this departure from the royal prerogative, which was believed to be another valuable trait derived from the ruler's selection by God as part of God's grand plan to rule over the subjects who lived in the land.

We secret friends may, from time to time, change our assignment by aligning ourselves to a different person, male or female, as some of us are female and some of us are male—but we do not always align with gender specific persons these days, because gender has become an imprecise label. We never have more than one attachment at a time. In that behavior, we are a person loyal—that is one of the planks in the structure of our credo. You see, most of us belong to the IOIF, the International Order of Imaginary Friends. And we adhere to its guiding code of ethics.

Perhaps our presence can be regarded as spiritual, much like a sacred and mysterious fog whispering through the mind of someone who senses its closeness, its immediacy, and its fresh importance to their life.

* * *

That was when I heard Reverend Moss' voice asking, "Are you my secret friend, my new helpmeet?"

I replied, "You may call me Heck. For that is my name, Reverend. I am here when you need to talk. That is, the times when you are receptive to my comments, which will always be directed to you for your benefit, at least my thoughts will be intended in that governing spirit, even if you discount or resist my current message."

"Do I put you in my prayers?"

"Wheez!" I exclaimed quietly to myself, and then, recovering my composure, told the Reverend, "Not necessarily. Prayers, unlike our conversations, are sacred, and flow between you and the prayer recipient."

"God, of course."

"I suppose, if you believe. Or to whomsoever of God's intermediaries to whom you may direct your reverence, your pleading, your beseeching, your message."

"I believe."

"Good for you."

"Don't you?"

"Yes, Reverend, in carrying out my role." Being spiritual, I believe in the abstract." I paused before explaining to my charge, "Reverend, I will leave you now, but I will resurface when you want my input."

"My sermon…." He grew silent, pondering. Soon he admitted, "I need guidance in composing. I must ferret out the sinners and address them, you see?"

Silence from me. This selection by me and by him is not going well.

CHAPTER 34

The Deacons

———

Six persons who, by title in ancient Greece, would be considered servants to the man who would have been in charge, leading the Deacons gathered in the upper room of a sanctuary. The Deacons to Reverend Moss, or so I learned, consisted of a woman, whose role was the organizer and perpetuator for the women's circles, groups of women with feminist callings who met frequently to review and discuss the words of the Bible as interpreted to reinforce their beliefs about the merits of female governance of the church and society in general. However, it had soon become apparent that such feminist leanings were contrary to official church doctrine, meaning the Reverend must, by church law, automatically disagree with many of his Deacons.

Another Deacon was the local school superintendent who was dedicated to performing religious education for the children of the congregational members. The third deacon lived on a nearby hilltop—an astronomer with telescopes galore who was intent on peering into outer space for signs of the One all-powerful deity, or possible other deities, along with alien civilizations throughout the universe. The fourth was a grocer whose shop supplied food for church dinners, as well as wine for sacraments. The sixth ran the nearby active adult retirement community, not affiliated with the church, whose occupants made up a contingent of the congregation, and who were divided into tiers of beliefs about life after death, each advocacy group holding meetings to discuss their take as to the dimensions of eternity.

I sensed the potential discordance among the Deacons and wondered how the Reverend was managing to manage his church and its many-faceted congregation. How could he structure sermons and personal visits with his members while recalling each of their unique personal agendas?

Becoming aware of the varied roster of folks around the Reverend, I asked him, "How do you relate to your members, there apparently being a wide spectrum of spiritual beliefs?"

"I'm needing guidance—your guidance."

"Tell me about your concerns."

The Reverend poured a fresh swig of his favorite Irish Scotch. Downing it with one satisfying gulp, he licked his lips and told me, "In seminary, we each took several classes in the practices of directing a congregation, keeping them focused on the dogma's religious messages. In other words, as pastor, I must stay in charge of the dialogue. The lesson for me as pastor, and therefore the mission of the congregation—is to squelch questions, and for heaven's sake discourage dissent. If they don't fall in line, then shame them, if you must, especially in front of the others."

"Military formations and protocol," I suggested.

The Reverend nodded.

Frankly, I must say, internally I cringed, but I didn't show my disappointment on his insistence on discouraging open religious dialogue. Yet it didn't take me much time to conclude that in my forthcoming experience with his religious group there would be no intellectual pursuits, no original interpretations of Bible stories, no searching for new thoughts, no new ideas, no fresh interpretations. I mean, after all, most of the Bible stories were going back into earlier times from Greece, Persia, Asia Minor and what is today Iraq. So, why not discuss that information and put a fresh slant on what the leaders of the dogma insist we believe today, to follow, and to stick with? For sure, there's nothing wrong with re-telling ancient stories and perhaps deriving spiritual guidance from them, but let's realize what it is we're subscribing to and subordinating our thoughts to.

I asked myself what was to become of the parishioners with questions, with ideas, with fresh slants on the ingrained stories? From where would come new inspirations? Soon I concluded, "Pity." For that is what a secret friend is for—that is his or her mission—to put stories, ideas and thoughts into a perspective, helping the principal to see himself or herself in a broader and brighter light. That is what I am good at. Those are my skills. That is my expertise. That is what I want to practice, pursue and promote, if I may try to express my feelings that way, and that was the announced end of my brief stint with Reverend Moss.

CHAPTER 35

Old White Men

——

Adrift in my rebellious discontent, I soon sensed vibes that I thought surely must be coming from a young woman. Now, how do you tell the gender of vibes?

The sex of thoughts? I have come to believe that indeed there are differences. Unique gender-driven differences. And what are they? Well, for one thing, female vibes start with "I", whereas male vibes begin with the problem needing to be fixed. But this set of thoughts were definitely female for they began with the question, "What am I going to do?"

I replied, "What would you like to do?"

"Kill all the men." She paused, then asked, "Are you male? Whoever you are."

"I'm Heck." I paused, soon adding, "I'm whatever you want me to be, as long as I can help you toward your goals, that is if you will share them with me."

Slowly, first thinking about my reply, then speaking to me directly, she said, "I want you to help me and my friends with our special landscape project." She laughed to herself and then to me, as if she had disclosed the secret plot in a complex novel.

"A special landscape project? Don't you simply plant, fertilize, water, and prune?"

"Normally."

"But this project of yours is not normal?"

"You got it. It's out of the norm, more or less." She waited, questioning, "Much like you must be, because I can't see you, but we are having a conversation nevertheless."

"Yes." Then I explained to her about the world of secret friends.

She replied, "Wow!" Thinking for a moment, she went on, "That sounds like the exciting world I want to travel to."

I assured her, "No travel required, for you are here now."

"Tell me, are you aging? I mean, how old are you anyway?"

"How old would you like me to be?"

"Not old. You see, I don't like things or people that are old."

"Why not?"

She insisted, "Because I am young."

"And you'd like me to be young, as well?"

"Of course."

"But not everyone is young. Some are older."

"Some people are really old. I mean old old. And I don't like old old men."

"Why just men?"

"Because men don't change, don't advance with wisdom, don't take on new roles, don't adopt new ideas. Old men are stuck in yesteryear, so to speak, reliving their careers, talking about their past accomplishments, which always include bragging about the women they have abused. Then they go on to tell how they have taken advantage of minorities in their business practices, and especially disclosing the deceptions embodied in their products…

all in their make rush to dominate others, whether they be men or women."

I asked, "What would you say if I told you I could well be in that age bracket?"

"But you're not...are you?"

"What if I were? That is the question, isn't it, and here you are talking to me as if I were equal in age with you —which is okay, because I can be your secret friend, and you can talk to me any way you wish to, and I'll respond to you, putting your response into perspective so that you can judge what you just said to me in your recent opinionated decree."

"You mean, you will often, or maybe even always disagree with me?"

"So, you don't want anyone to disagree with you?"

"Why would anyone want to disagree with me?

"You are right all the time."

"Of course."

"In that case, we must part, say goodbye to each other, I'm afraid."

"You must be old old to have that attitude."

To that, I came back quickly with, "You must be young young to have that attitude. Besides, my friend, I don't do closed minds, for I can't help trying to change a closed mind, or even regretting a closed mindset, for if the mind is closed, then there is no opening."

Silence ensued. Perhaps I was gone from her mind. Soon I heard a pleading, "Oh, please, Heck, don't go, I'm sorry. Please be patient with me."

"Patience is my trump card."

"I think I would welcome your thoughts about my landscape business."

"You think you would? Then please try me."

"It's an age and gender thing. You see, my cousin Hernando is graduating from high school. He has a scholarship to the state university in both chemistry and epidemiology."

"Nice."

"Yes. You see, he's come up with a fertilizer for use in my landscape business."

"And?"

"We have a grant from a population think tank—"

"—Name?"

"Fertility Unlimited."

"A think tank with a mission."

"In a way."

"How so?"

"Well, it is run by women."

"And what are all you women thinking these days?"

She hesitated to tell me. For a moment, that is. But then....

"Out with it," I urged. I waited.

Soon came, "It's complicated."

"What is not these days?" I added, "My friend, I thrive on complicated things." I added, "Try me." I waited, then added, "Please."

Slowly she said, "I call it a conspiracy."

"Can you define this term 'conspiracy?'"

She stumbled out with, "Well, if all the people in the world were arrayed against you, would you be facing a conspiracy?"

"Are they assembled against you?"

"Not me…against men, yes men"

"Then would you call it a gender threat?"

She nodded. "And I don't know what I can do, because this product, this scheme, will be fatal, and I mean deadly."

"For men?"

Slowly and quietly and with a nod, she said, "Maybe. Yes.

Some, I think. Maybe others…I just don't know, but that's what they are saying."

"They? Who is they? Tell me, how will It work?"

"Can't say. I don't know the details. But I do know what they are saying."

Softly I prodded, "You are telling me It is a deadly conspiracy plot, but you can't tell me what is involved in this…whatever it is, or who is telling you these things? Or how it will work? Or what is the real true-life danger to people?"

"To a lot of people!"

"And your landscaping business is somehow involved?"

"Not so willingly…but by being intimidated…."

"Threatened?"

"By the consequences if I don't play along."

"That makes you a co-conspirator."

"Yes, that's where I need your help…or someone's help."

"Can't you simply run away…punt, so to speak?"

"I'd lose my business."

"To whom?"

"To them, all of them." I could sense she was beginning to cry. For the moment, I was baffled as to what to say, how to try to comfort her, how to find out more.

* * *

Then I recalled her cousin Hernando and his high school chemistry project, or was it a discovery? And did she say he was being backed somehow, financially I supposed, by some group? Were they venture capitalists? Or were they a foreign entity bent on some nefarious mission?

"I asked her to tell me more about Hernando.

"He's in hiding. Run away. I don't know where he is. He won't email me or return my cell calls."

"What more can you tell me about him?"

"He is really into weird experiments."

"For example."

"He was studying body temperatures of different groups of students and people. He got mentioned in scientific journals for his research and ideas. And a number of people overwhelmed him, one after the other, with contracts. For example, one day he told me that groups of people—categorized by their gender, interest, what have you, will have slightly different body temperatures. Heretofore you can target groups by categorizing their temperatures. So, for his fertilizer, for example, my landscape business, he was able to make it safe for certain animals by excluding their temperatures, so he could direct the fertilizer at certain groups of people using the same technique of categorizing their body temperatures." She paused. "How sinister!"

"You mean….my God…exterminating them?"

"Yes, you've got to somehow intervene…stop him." She was now pleading with me, "Stop them."

"How?"

"Indeed. He should be locked up somewhere where he can't do such things. And just maybe that's where he has confined himself… But meanwhile, this fertilizer is out there with its threats, and that's where I am being intimidated to either keep quiet or go along with it…them…for a financial reward, that is, if I do so. Otherwise… lights out for me."

"But why would anyone want to wipe out a certain category of people?'

She laughed uproariously. You are innocent, my secret friend. Don't you read the papers, listen to the TV, read the rumors? Heed the hedonistic?"

"For example?" I implored. "Give me examples…please."

"We're going to a meeting. You'll get the idea. I want you to see and hear and then tell me what you think."

It was my duty to comply with her wish, and so off we went.

* * *

The meeting location was as unusual as the topics being discussed by the mostly women present. I felt out of place, but I was committed to observe, which meant, at first, listening and then, I supposed, commenting about the statements and opinions being expressed.

I felt uncomfortable in the room, crowded as it was, for everyone seemed to be talking, few listening. "Without men…especially older men…they're all so biased…so opinionated about every subject…overtalking…trying to tell us what to think and why."

"They don't care what we women think."

"It's as if we don't matter…except—"

"—Unless it's something to do with sex."

From the ceiling and on the walls of the room were placards and banners, some printed, some hand-made, some colorful, some stark, but each either extolling women or else deriding men. I was glad I couldn't be seen. One section of the room its walls changing from pink to gray, was devoted to signs deriding old age, proclaiming that old people were "in the way." "They cost us a lot of money to provide for them in their doddering old age, and they use up so much space and personnel in hospitals and clinics, taking resources away from maternity, from babies, from pediatrics, from children." Another sign said: "And from abortions and fertility clinics and research." "It's all about men, old men."

"See what I mean?" she asked, obviously awaiting my comments.

"There's no room of time or even an invitation for conversation. Everyone has their mind made up."

She added, "And their take on body temperature."

"Meaning?"

"Temperature registers with gender and age and then interacts with this new fertilizer."

I was stunned, even though I had sensed, to my chagrin, that's the direction in which our whole conversation, indeed the thoughts and perhaps even the contemplations of the people—the women in this room—was heading.

Fearing her answer, I pressed, "Are you telling me the women here advocate wiping out an entire segment of the population?"

"Old men, mostly white men," she quicky said, hiding her face from showing emotion.

"But why?"

"It's been too long,"

"What can you possibly mean?"

She took us aside into an adjacent room where there was little spill over from the commotion of the larger room and the conversations and signs displayed there. She said, "These women...I mean almost all of them, I've come to find out by listening but not necessarily agreeing with them...go back to the founding of this country and slavery."

"Many are black...."

"...yes, of course."

"Slavery was evil," I suggested, to her nod of agreement.

She said, "Three-fifths was what the old white men of the north allowed the south to count their slaves and get Congressional representation from that number plus their white folk. Those white men disallowed the humanity of the blacks, the slaves."

"Yes, that is what took place in the Constitution when it was finally adopted all those many years ago….1780's something. I'd have to look up the exact date."

"Whatever the year, these women want to trash the country today and all the old white men alive today for allowing that to have happened."

"But that was 200-plus some years ago," I stated emphatically. Thinking more about it, I slowly added, "And that's what they're planning to do with this new fertilizer, as controlled by body temperature of old white men as it is being applied to their gardens and lawns by your landscape company?"

"And others, as well, not just mine."

"But you don't have to go along with it. I mean, you can walk away from this scheme and not do it, not use their fertilizer, can't you?"

She hid her face from me. She was crying. I waited. Tears. I felt the emotions exuding from her, and I felt sorry for her. Finally, I prodded, repeating my question, "Can't you?"

Slowly she shook her head. In a moment, she pleaded, her voice lowered to whisper level, "You have to help me…my dear secret friend Heck."

I told her right away, "I want to, but you have to explain more about your predicament, so I can react to it and hopefully suggest something—"

"—More than just one thing…."

"Yes of course, but first you must tell me about these pressures you are feeling."

* * *

Some time elapsed as I waited for her, through another bout of tears, to try to explain to me. Finally, she began, "You see, my

mother has dementia. She now lives in a very expensive full-care facility. I mean round the clock attention, for she's liable to simply walk
out the door and continue walking, heaven knows where she intends
to go. After their staff had to go searching for her every evening for a
week, they moved her to a round-the-clock area of the large facility,
where doors are locked and patients are watched 24/7 by staff members. They can roam around inside two rooms, watch TV, play board
games…you know, harmless activities. But at least they are on the
premises, safe, and not in any physical danger."

"Nice," I commented. "sounds expensive…on your part, I
mean, unless you have siblings who will help out…money wise, I
mean, as well as help in looking after her."

"No, none. There's not even my father who passed away several years ago."

"His estate?"

"Minimal." She thought, adding, "Nowhere near enough for
my mother's care."

"So, how do you—"

"—That's my dilemma. Do you simply say to your parent or
your spouse or your relative, "I'm sorry, but we're out of funds? I did
manage to get you a sleeping bag so when you're out on the streets
you can sleep in it with some degree of comfort. I'll try to check in on
you two or three times a week, as long as I know where on the streets
or in which shelter to look."

I choked up.

She went on in presumed advice for her mother, 'I'll monitor
your meds and continue to pick them up at the pharmacy."

"Stop," I implored. "You are obviously not at that juncture, or
are you?"

"No, and there is my dilemma."

"How so?"

"My mother has an angel."

"From the clouds on high or from a charity here on Earth?"

"Neither."

"Where, then?"

Hesitatingly, she began to unfurl her story: "There was a family with three young sisters. Their father was a druggist in a small rural town in Georgia. He was curious about sedatives, pain killers, and other related compounds that he experimented with and could give to local folks who were in pain. Over time he developed a drug that worked quite effectively. Word got out in the town and around the county. His product was in demand. In those days there was no federal licensing procedure, so he just compounded quantities and sold them to doctors and other druggists in the area."

In fascination, I listened, imaging this druggist deep in the rural South, imagining how gratified he must have felt with his achievements and with the knowledge of the relief that he must have been able to provide for certain afflicted folks in the area. "Go on, I urged."

"The three sisters worshipped their father and his dedication to help humanity. They admired his enthusiasm for medicines and began to devote their lives to the furtherance of what eventually in our day and even earlier, became the field of medical science."

"They were a loyal family," I surmised.

"Yes." Then she grew quiet.

"What happened?" I asked, anticipating a change in the flow of the story.

She continued, "Well, you see, the mother of the three sisters was African American. Her skin was lighter, and her racial legacy was, at first, not known. But now that the father of the sisters was beginning to gain notoriety and the drug had become so popular, racial prejudice began to surface. The cry went out among the white population that no blacks were to be given the drug. Protests were publicized against doctors and druggists who were giving the drug to blacks; crosses were burned; hate and racial bigotry began to run rampant."

"How awful," I stated

She nodded and went on, "However, the father had gone to the university in order to qualify for his degree in pharmacy. There, as a student, he had met the dean of the law school, with whom he now consulted."

"And?"

"The dean had kept in contact with one of his female graduates who was now with a large drug company in the North, with whom he spoke."

"And a long story short?"

She smiled, finally, and I was relieved that she was pleased to be telling me this story. She went on, "This drug company looked into the pain-relieving drug that the father had concocted and, incidentally, patented."

"Good move."

She smiled and continued, "After their investigation and negotiation, which was lengthy, the drug company finally paid the three sisters, who were acting on behalf of their father who by now was elderly, a huge sum of money plus, to boot, overriding royalties on future sales of the drug. In short, the three sisters, acting for their father, became super wealthy."

"I have a feeling there is more…."

"Yes, and here goes: In later life the three sisters argued over their share of the money and on how to spend and invest it. One sister finally bought out the other two and, over a few years, became one of the wealthiest women in America."

"Nice for her," I suggested.

"Maybe," she mumbled, "but not without controversy."

"How so?"

"This wealthy sister became a strong feminist and, in addition an advocate for blacks and all minorities in America. With her wealth, she backed all sorts of radical solutions io what she perceived as the major problems facing the country."

"Can you give me examples of her beliefs…the causes for which she is advocating and maybe even funding?"

"I thought you might not want to go there."

"But I do, please, as I feel whatever it is is causing you this awful angst."

"Well, you see, she is the primary backer of the fertilizer company that I must use to fertilize my gardens. If I refuse her support by not buying my fertilizer from her company, then there goes the financial support for my mother's expensive dementia care."

I took this all in and then asked for my own understanding, "You're telling me this woman advocates killing off white men? For these would be the only targets of the poisoned fertilizer."

She nodded and then quickly hid her face. "And, Heck, you see, I've become a pawn in her demographic scheme to redo the makeup of the population of our country in order to follow the dictates of her warped sense of whom she wants running our society— women and minorities, not old white men."

Not being an old white man, I felt no discrimination… and yet…what did I feel for sure? I felt something. However secret friends are not designed to feel, only to react. But maybe my reaction was part of how I had begun to feel, sensing and then soon deeply feeling the prejudice coming from this wealthy older woman. I began to wonder if she had the benefit of a secret friend advising her, feeding back to her a summary of her own ever-so biased opinions, so that she could place them in a larger perspective, one that would give her a historical outlook on life and, hopefully, a less egregious one. After all, the role of a secret friend is not necessarily to change the opinions of a person but to characterize his or her opinions so that they reflect a mirror of one's self, laying bare the possible roots of prejudice and bias. If the opinions survive this examination, then so be it, but at least they would have had the benefit of circumspection, thanks to her secret friend.

Would that everyone could avail themselves of the benefits of having a secret friend. But, wait, how many of us cadres of secret friends are there? Are there enough of us to satisfy the world-wide demand? Probably not. I belong to the IOIF, but I have no idea how many members we have, or if we recruit new members or even keep track of existing members.

Yet, just think back in history if leaders had had secret friends. Oh, maybe they did, and that was the problem with them. No, I don't believe that. For if, every political leader had had an imaginary friend to put his or her opinions and decisions into perspective, maybe history would have been a lot different, a lot better, fewer wars, more people living out their lives than being killed in war's battles or in holocaust-like wipe-outs.

Had Hitler had a Jew for a secret friend, telling him that what he was saying and doing was going to lead to disaster, and had he listened, the world would be a much different place today, wouldn't it?

Had the Popes had secret friends telling him the Crusades were wrong and would have only added to misery and death for millions of men, women, and children…maybe the bitterness toward other religions beliefs would be less, more tolerant.

Be that as it may, truth be told, things were not that way. So, my fantasy evaporating, what was I to tell my companion to help guide her through her dilemma?

She was begging me for guidance, but my role was not in providing answers but rather to mirror her own biases and put her dilemmas into perspective that might allow her to devise her own solutions. After all, secret friends don't maintain a library of answers from which to check out self-help books, nor do we write them.

So, I was stumped. Stymied. Lost for words. Wait! That is no good. For an instant, I thought I personally needed my own secret friend, someone I could rely upon for assistance.

But now, once again, she was calling upon me with yet another plea for guidance. Her mother's expensive care; her deadly fertilizer; her dire financial struggle; her own biases. What was her way out? If there was any way. Was her mother doomed to lose her vital care? Was my charge to cause the deaths of hundreds, yes even thousands of older white men? Whence my self-regard for myself for failing her? My self-esteem?

If Hitler had had an imaginary friend, a Jew, who was called upon to advise, what would his failure have done to the imaginary friend? Kaput! A camp? And that would have been that for the imaginary friend. Pity for him. Pity for his charge. Pity for history. Pity for the millions of victims. Pity for the soldiers and their families. Pity all around.

In like manner, was that to be it for my worried friend? No. Surely, I must do something! With urgency. Hesitatingly I tried, "Tell me, please, do you belong to a trade organization of landscape maintenance companies?"

"Yes."

"Is there someone there, a leading and respected member perhaps, who could step in and help set up fertilizer standards that would exclude the chemical makeup of this deadly product aimed at older white men you are being intimidated to acquire and soon be required to spread?"

She replied right away, "Yes. The state organization has a chemist who is supposed to approve each fertilizer."

"Talk to him."

"It's a her."

"Better yet. Call her," I suggested, "Can you ask her to comment on the ingredients, take a close chemical look at its safety, its effects on humans…on men in particular."

"She'll think I'm nuts, out of my mind when I tell her my suspicions."

"What do you care what she thinks, as long as she does what you ask her to do. With her results, you will promptly report her warning to the entire trade group. You and she will ask, no demand, that the organization ban the product's use."

Silence. And then she protested, "But the evil rich woman, once she finds out, will surely intervene."

I suggested to my charge, "By then, it'll be too late, for in the meantime you will have gone to the media with the findings and to all organizations presumably there to protect older people from all sorts of nefarious schemes, asking for their support."

To my complete surprise, it took her only a moment to quip in a decisive and conclusive tone, "Once again, older white men will be saved."

The message in her voice was so final, so "end of storyish" that I was dumbfounded. I knew not what to say. I struggled for words. I struggled for a sense of her mind—hopefully revised by my idea to help her solve her problem. Perhaps she'd rather have the problem than the satisfaction and comfort of a solution. For sure, such was her choice, her decision. Abruptly then, like a radio station gone off the air, the music ended, the signal was only the silence of a connection lost.

And I was adrift in a void, that old familiar and unwelcome black hole of loneliness.

* * *

I can't compute how much time passed, for to secret friends like me time is as irrelevant as my sartorial choices. I waited patiently, although maybe not so patiently, hoping for the void to pass away, to eventually disappear like the darkest of nights giving way to new light.

"Thank Heaven," I felt as a flicker of light in the form of a fresh voice reached me through the dark. It was asking, hopefully asking me, "When did life change to advance with the brightness and variety of color, technicolor, instead of everything, every scene, being dull and lifeless black and white?"

I replied, "There's always been color."

"No, no," the voice declared, bordering on finality, "From the get-go, every day was black and white. Then something changed, and suddenly one day we had color."

"The movies," I suggested.

The voice acted as if I had opened one of the curtains on one of the closets of life. It said, "Yes, thinking more about the subject, I do agree. You are right." Then the voice demanded to know, "Are you always right?"

Hesitatingly, I replied, "I try to be. But I know why you are asking about black and white, for there was a time when I and many others thought that when the Puritans landed in the New World and built their houses, they were always white—I mean both the Puritans and the houses."

"And?"

I went on, "Then I talked with a Colonial historian and asked about my view of Colonial Massachusetts. She assured me that houses had been painted in startling and varied colors, and that the people, while their skins were white, the folks who had been there since time immemorial were shades of brown, so that the people were a kaleidoscope of dancing colors, what with their attire and their skins, plus the variety of their clothing and all the various colors of their houses, variety was the theme of Colonial Massachusetts."

"As it is today in modern-day America."

"And the world," I added, then hesitatingly asked, "And what do you do in your colorful real life?"

"I ask questions. You see, I want to get it all straight...before...."

"Before what?"

"Before it's too late to care about the detail of the ingredients that make up the answers."

"When is it too late to ask and to care?"

"That's a medical question, coming from medical science, ranging from blood tests and too many other tests to mention or even to know in advance—it's up to medical science from there on out. And when medical science begins to ask its laundry list of questions, then it is too late for me to explore answers to all my additional questions."

"So, ask away."

The voice thought and finally agreed, "Okay. Next query: why do people believe what they believe, what they espouse in conversations, what they want to talk about—well, I mean are they echoing some conspiracy theory? I'd like to know what goes 'round and 'round in their heads, you see."

"I do. I'd like to know, too."

"And how do we find out?"

"Look at opinion polls…."

"I didn't need those when I was building houses. I looked at sales and at properties on the market, their prices, their features. Much like looking at people today and asking questions."

"And you sold houses?"

"Yes, sooner or later. There is always a demand for housing."

I offered, "I knew a home builder years ago." I paused, awaiting input, but got none, then added, "What did you do after building houses?"

"I decided to write a novel, and did, and then another. That's what got me into asking questions about how people think. As well as just general questions."

I asked, "How did that endeavor work out for you?"

His voice growing enthusiastic, he replied, "Great, at least as far as I was concerned. I mean, the words came like the designs of the houses came to me—pictures in my mind in the form of paragraphs and chapters, plus windows into the minds of each of my characters. My characters and my plots raised significant literary questions, offered the tension of a good novel and each one read well, in my opinion. That is, after I edited them extensively. All this, you see, during a period of hard work and pleasure during some 10 years." He became silent.

"But?" I prompted.

Dejectedly he said, "I couldn't sell any of my manuscripts to a major publisher."

I asked the obligatory question of "why not?"

He replied quickly, as if he wanted to change the subject, with one word, "Age."

"Yours?"

"Yes. Mine…and theirs."

I was having trouble understanding, and told him so. "What does age have to do with writing and selling a good novel to the publisher and then the publisher selling the novel to bookstore and they to readers?"

"Good question."

I allowed, "Yes, I know it is." I Pressed, "And your answer is?"

He said, "I've always believed in that scenario…ever since I was a kid reading books. So, here's what happened to me in my efforts to sell my manuscript to literary agents. But let me tell you first, to reach the major publishers, you have to go through an agent, for publishers will only look at a manuscript submitted by an agent—not directly from an author. So, I sent what are called query letters to a list of agents. It is the letter in which you have to tell the agent about your qualifications to write the novel, your background—and through it all of the disclosure, tidbits such as your age and gender choice are, of course, revealed."

"What happened? I mean, did you get responses to your battery of letters sent out to agents?"

"I was turned down every time, that is, when I did receive responses. More than half the time, I got no replies."

"But you didn't give up?"

"Right. I thought about a different marketing strategy. I changed, by taking my name off the manuscript and making up a pen name. Then I told agents the real writer was really my younger sister, who was confined to a wheel chair from permanent injuries received from physical abuses by her former husband. I then decided to personally deliver the manuscript to agents in New York—that's where most of them are, as well as the major publishers."

"And you did just that?"

"You bet. And in spades. I went to Manhattan, manuscript copies in hand, and a list of the few agents who had responded to me.

In advance, I wrote to them, reiterating that I was planning to deliver the manuscript personally to them on behalf of my sister during my forthcoming visit to Manhattan."

"And you did this?"

"Yes. Once there, I tried to get to know first one, then another agent on a first name basis."

"I'm anxious to know your results?"

He began to unravel what became a short story of his big city adventure: "At the first agent's address high up in a Manhattan office building, I was greeted by a uniformed and weaponized guard whose life seemed to depend upon turning me away after she had called the agent's in-house phone number and apparently did not receive a pass-through clearance for me. I protested that I had written the agent in advance, but the guard said "no." To boot she was becoming belligerent. With her left hand firmly grasping her weapon and a look of satisfying revenge spreading across her face, I hastily turned and took the down elevator.

Next, I did meet an agent in person, but by then it was late in the day. She was rather attractive. Having read her background ahead of time, I learned she was a graduate of Wellesley and was newly learning the ropes of her business from this large agency. Well, as people were leaving the office for the day, I asked her to dinner that evening. She agreed. We arranged to meet later in a nearby Manhattan restaurant known for its literary fame."

"Good move," I interrupted, suggesting progress in his mission.

"I thought so. Sitting down for drinks at the bar next to the dining area, we talked about writing. I let her know I had helped my sister write the manuscript. The agent began leafing through the manuscript that I had handed her earlier.

"Getting on good with her." I remarked.

"Yes, but as we got into the mission of the moment, I mistakenly let it be known that I, as the real author, was bent in making an agent contact for myself, and that I had no sister. It was all a fiction, a fiction writer's lark."

I commented, "Unfortunate disclosure, so I would guess." I waited in silence, dreading the next happening. Nevertheless, I began to query, "So, what—"

"—Well, we were sitting next to the swinging door that passes wait persons from the restaurant into the kitchen and out again. Just at that moment, it swung open, casting the brighter kitchen light onto me. Seeing me in this new and brighter light, she burst out with, "My God, you're an Old White Man! You'll never get published. She swigged down the rest of her sauvignon blanc in an impressive elbow-up maneuver and, now yelling at me, delivered her professional female agent literati judgment, "You'll ruin me in my new profession! When word gets out that I've met with an old white male author, I'll become the laughing stock of the literati, probably relegated to working in the mail room in my agency."

"I immediately protested, 'I don't get it.'"

"She took brief pity on me being from the literati hinterland, and she sensed the need to make some sort of explanation, which she fired at me, her face turning red with indignation as she went on, 'The publishing industry today is not like it used to be, dominated in those days by older white men. Today the decisions are made by young women of several ethnic origins, generally under 40 years of age. As it is with agencies and publishers, it's a women's business these days and men are not welcome!'"

"She picked herself up, through the plate of hors d'oeuvre at me, grabbed her bag and stormed out of the bar, leaving me with the bar tab.

"She shouted after herself so that the entire room caught her literary lecture, "Everybody in this business these days is female. None of us want to read about old white men, nor do our readers, nor do the women buyers for bookstores or libraries. No one is interested in old white men or what you write or what you say. Not anymore! The world has changed and you might as well get used to it."

* * *

I queried, "What do you take away from your experience?"

"Now? Maybe, as I said, it is getting too late in life...."

I suggested, "Perhaps if you made out a list—and it might be long—of questions you want to ask yourself, me, and everyone you come in contact with...then you wouldn't run out of questions, and medical science would never dare usurp your mental capacity... would not dare divert your attention away from what was vital for you to master...to know." Then I suggested, "And you could write about your answers...through the minds of your characters."

"You know, you have good ideas, good knowledge."

"Thank you. It's my job."

"Which is?"

I dodged the question, not sure how to reply. I thought for a moment. Silence, until he reiterated, "Which is?"

I tried, "I see my job, if you want to label It as such, being to critique the mind of my charge and empathize with their situations in life."

He jumped in, adding, "And then to try, given my experiences in business and in society, to tell their stories in intriguing and tension-filled tales that convey to readers the hopes and fears of real—what I call imaginary or fictitious lives."

"Sounds familiar," I managed slowly adding, "I think our paths may have crossed some years ago." I waited.

He said, "But we're just having an innocent little conversation. Conversations don't come back years later, do they? They can't reappear? Can they? From out of the wild untamed blue of space?"

"Another of your questions?"

"Yes." He waited, adding, "And the answer is?"

"It may be possible, that is, if anything is possible…anything."

"Your name?"

"What's yours?"

THE END

AUTHOR'S END NOTE

———

"The Last Communist Town in Italy"—Pietrasanta was where I began the year 2020 while visiting Helen's granddaughter on her first birthday. There, I began to compose "The Idea which Thinks Itself" (C. F. Hegel, 1830). I wrote every morning, either in the Bar Michelangelo overlooking the Piazza or in the three-story walk-up Bibliotheca adjacent to the 13th century Duomo.

The novel is based on my experience as a home builder in the Great Central Valley of California some years ago.

FURTHER READING

———

Jon Foyt's published novels and essays are described on his website at **www.jonfoyt.com**, from where books can be ordered from Amazon and bookstores.

ABOUT JON FOYT

—

A native of Indianapolis, Jon graduated from Shortridge High School, concurrently with soon-to-be acclaimed novelist Dan Wakefield and U.S. Senator-to-be Richard Lugar, and in the wake of Kurt Vonnegut. He studied journalism and geography at Stanford University and then earned an MBA on the Farm. He served in the Army in Military Intelligence, followed by careers in electronics, radio broadcasting, banking, and real estate development.

In 1951, he married Lois Rehfeldt. They had three children: Jennifer, Weston, and Randolph, followed by eight grandchildren and two great grandsons.

In 1987, he returned to academic at the University of Georgia to work on a degree in Historic Preservation. He has lived in most regions of the U.S. and in England. In 1977, Lois returned to Stanford for her degree in Feminist Studies.

In 2011, Lois passed away, and Jon moved to Rossmoor, an active adult community in Walnut Creek, California. There, he writes a political column for the weekly Rossmoor News and continues to produce novels.

Foyt has been a distance runner, having completed 60 marathons and a lot of half-marathons and shorter races. He now enjoys walking around Rossmoor and on local trails

He can be contacted at **jonfoyt@mac.com** or on his website at **www.jonfoyt.com**

www.ingramcontent.com/pod-product-compliance
Lightning Source LLC
Chambersburg PA
CBHW020559250626
47154CB00004B/1281